mary-kate olsen ashley olsen

so little time

Check out these other great
so little time
titles:

Book 1: **how to train a boy**

Book 2: **instant boyfriend**

Coming soon!

Book 4: **just between us**

mary-kate olsen **ashley** olsen

so little time

too good to be true

By Nancy Butcher

Based on the teleplay by Marcy Vosburgh

HarperEntertainment
An Imprint of HarperCollinsPublishers

A PARACHUTE PRESS BOOK

A PARACHUTE PRESS BOOK

Parachute Publishing, L.L.C.
156 Fifth Avenue, Suite 302
New York, NY 10010

Published by
HarperEntertainment
An *Imprint of* HarperCollins*Publishers*
10 East 53rd Street, New York, NY 10022-5299

SO LITTLE TIME books are created and produced by Parachute Press, L.L.C., in cooperation with Dualstar Publications, a division of Dualstar Entertainment Group, Inc., published by HarperEntertainment, an imprint of HarperCollins Publishers.

ISBN 0-06-008805-2

HarperCollins®, **♦**®, and HarperEntertainment™ are trademarks of HarperCollins Publishers Inc.

First printing: May 2002

Printed in the United States of America

Visit HarperEntertainment on the World Wide Web at
www.harpercollins.com

10 9 8 7 6 5 4 3

chapter
one

"**W**ow, Argentina," fourteen-year-old Riley Carlson murmured. "Can you believe Ms. D'Amico is moving there? Do you think there's even a remote possibility she'd invite us for a little vacation?"

"I *wish*," Riley's twin sister, Chloe, replied. "Then we'd have a reason to buy a bunch of new clothes. Sundresses, shorts, Capri pants, tankinis…"

"So true!" Riley agreed. Her sister was always thinking about clothes. Of course, Riley liked marathon shopping just as much as Chloe did. It must be a genetic thing, she thought. I mean, our parents *are* fashion designers, after all.

Riley and Chloe were freshmen at West Malibu High, and yesterday their ceramics teacher, Ms. D'Amico, had suddenly announced that she was moving to South America.

Now, on Saturday morning, Riley and Chloe were at

the dining room table, lingering over breakfast and going over the school's list of elective classes. They were trying to pick out a last-minute replacement for ceramics.

Chloe slid the list across the table to Riley. "Let's go with something fun," she suggested. "How about environmental cleanup and conservation?"

Riley took a bite of cinnamon toast and frowned at the list. "I don't get it. What's so fun about *that*?"

"You've got to read between the lines." Chloe grinned. "'Environmental cleanup' means you go to the beach with your friends and pick up a few empty cans."

Riley laughed. She glanced out the window at the long stretch of beach just beyond their house. The early-morning sun shimmered on the water. A group of cute boys jogged by. Hmm, I wouldn't mind spending some extra time on the beach, she decided.

Riley heard high heels clattering briskly down the stairs. She turned and saw a blur of red disappear through the kitchen doorway. Hurricane Mom, she thought.

Their dog, Pepper, followed at Mom's heels, clearly expecting breakfast. Pepper had big brown eyes and white fur with a sprinkling of black here and there.

"Good morning, Mom!" Riley called out.

There was a noisy crash of pots and plates, Pepper began to bark, then, "Ow! Morning, girls!" Mom called.

Riley and Chloe exchanged a glance and shook their heads.

[<u>Riley</u>: So you're reading this and wondering what's the deal with our mom, right? Well, Mom's kind of intense. Totally busy all the time. And maybe a little distracted, too. She and our dad used to run their fashion design business together. But Dad's kind of the opposite of my mom. A let's-play-it-by-ear kind of guy, you know? Very laid back. A few months ago they separated— both personally and professionally. Now Mom and Dad actually get along. But Mom runs the business on her own, which means that she's even more stressed out and hyper than she normally is.]

Seconds later, Macy Carlson emerged from the kitchen. She had a cup of coffee in one hand, a Palm Pilot in the other, and a bagel wedged between her teeth. She was dressed in a formfitting red suit that complemented her brown eyes and short brown hair.

"How are you two doing this morning?" Mrs. Carlson asked. But with the bagel in her mouth, it came out, "Har are oo woo ooing is orning?"

"Put *down* the bagel, ma'am," Chloe said in her best police officer voice.

"Orry!" Mrs. Carlson slid into a chair at the head of the table. She set down her coffee cup and Palm Pilot, then plucked the bagel out of her teeth and balanced it on top of the coffee cup. "There, that's better. Sorry to be in such a rush," she said breathlessly, "but I have a model coming for a fitting in ten minutes. I've got a meeting at nine o'clock with the head buyer at Generation, then a photo shoot at ten. And then, let's see, there's some fashion-show benefit-lunch thing I have to go to. At noon or one. Or is that happening *tomorrow*?" She picked up her Palm Pilot and started punching buttons.

"Mom, slow down," Riley said. She poured her a glass of juice. "Here, have some mango juice. I think it's supposed to be calming or something."

"No time for calm," Mrs. Carlson said, jabbing at her Palm Pilot. "How are you girls, anyway? Getting ready for school? What's new? Fill me in."

"Mom, it's Saturday," Riley reminded her. She pointed to her pink pajama bottoms and matching tank top. "Didn't you notice that Chloe and I are still in our jams? We were just trying to decide on our new electives. Ms. D'Amico's moving away, so we have to come up with something to replace ceramics class by Monday."

Chloe held up the class list. "We were thinking environmental cleanup and conservation might be cool."

Mrs. Carlson nodded. "Uh-huh, sounds good. Just stay away from any toxic spills. You don't want to sprout an extra nose!" She let out a peal of laughter.

"Ew!" Chloe cried. She reached up and touched her nose.

Just then, the back door swung open and Tedi breezed in. Tedi was a model Mrs. Carlson often worked with. She was tall and thin, and had long black hair.

Without saying hello, Tedi made a beeline for the telephone, which was on the counter. She picked it up and began dialing. "Need the phone," she said without looking up. "Agent beeped while I was jogging."

Pepper burst out of the kitchen and started yelping. Riley leaned down to pet her. "It's okay. It's just Tedi," she whispered. Pepper stopped barking and sat at Riley's feet.

Riley checked out Tedi's outfit. The woman was wearing black jogging shorts with a beeper hooked to the waistband, a gray and white tank top…and high heels.

I must have missed that trend, Riley thought. Who wore high heels to run?

Mrs. Carlson seemed to notice the same thing at the same time. "Um, Tedi? I know this may seem like a stupid question, and maybe I'm just an old-fashioned gal, but how can you possibly run in four-inch heels?"

Tedi shrugged. "How can I *not*? Someone might see me." She turned her attention to the phone. "Hi, it's Tedi. Uh-huh. Uh-huh. Uh-huh." Her eyes lit up. "What? Really?" She let out a piercing squeal and hung up the phone. "I got that commercial for wrinkle cream!" she announced.

"You don't have wrinkles," Mrs. Carlson said, giving Tedi the once-over.

Tedi rolled her eyes. "Well, duh, it's not as if the cream actually works."

Riley looked over the class list again. "Hey, Tedi, help us pick a good elective. Let's see, there's basic nutrition, wood shop, financial planning…" She paused. "Hmm, financial planning…I do need to save money for some new CDs."

Tedi leaned across the table. "Like anyone needs to know that stuff," she said. "Why don't they teach the important things, like tipping so your bags are the first ones off the plane, or how to look wind-blown when it's dead calm?"

Mrs. Carlson took a sip of her coffee. "While those are excellent skills," she told Tedi, "you have to remember, not everyone is a supermodel."

"Whatever. Does your school offer a class in how-to-date-for-jewelry?" Tedi asked Riley and Chloe. She held out her right hand, which sported a platinum ring with a sapphire the size of Neptune.

"Oh, wow!" Riley gasped. She had never seen a gem so big and sparkly. "That thing is huge."

Mrs. Carlson sighed and picked up the class list. She flipped through the pages briskly. "Here," she said, stopping on one. "How about intro to sewing? Or basic cooking, that's a good one! Cooking is a wonderful skill. There's nothing like being able to put together a well-balanced meal." She took a big bite of her bagel.

"Sierra's in that sewing class," Riley remembered. Sierra Pomeroy was one of Riley's closest friends. "We could make some cool outfits together."

"I think Amanda signed up for cooking," Chloe added. Amanda Gray was one of Chloe's friends. "Maybe I could fine-tune my smoothie-making talents. I don't know why we didn't think of this before, Riley!"

The sisters took the list from Mrs. Carlson and pored over the descriptions of the two classes. The more Riley thought about it, the more sewing sounded like fun. Chloe seemed pretty psyched about cooking, too.

"It's decided, then," Riley said. "Sewing and cooking!"

"Great! Wonderful! Speaking of sewing…" Mrs. Carlson turned to Tedi. "Let's do your fitting right away."

The phone rang. Pepper started barking and running around the room.

"I've got it." Mrs. Carlson jumped up from her chair.

Before Mom could reach the phone, Manuelo came rushing through the kitchen doorway. "I'll get it, I'll get it," he called out in his thick Spanish accent. He picked it up on the fourth ring. "Hello?"

Manuelo was the Carlsons' cook and housekeeper. Actually, he was way more than that. In the last fourteen years he'd become part of the family, helping Riley and Chloe with their homework, teaching them how to play pool, and giving them advice on friends, teachers, clothes, and more.

"Yes, this is the Carlson residence," Manuelo was saying to the person on the other end. "Yes, Mrs. Carlson is here. Would you like to speak to her?" He covered the mouthpiece with one hand. "Miss Macy, it's

Maria Rodriguez from the *Malibu Herald*," he whispered. He added, "Who wants some zucchini waffles for breakfast? It's a brand-new recipe I've been working on."

"Zucchini waffles? Hmm, I don't know," Chloe said, looking uncertain.

"Never mind the zucchini waffles. *Malibu Herald*? What do they want?" Mrs. Carlson demanded.

"I don't know—something about an interview," Manuelo said, shrugging. "For your information, the zucchini is a delicious vegetable," he told Chloe.

"Interview?" Mrs. Carlson grabbed the phone from Manuelo. "Hello? Yes, this is Macy Carlson...."

Riley leaned over to Chloe. "Mom's kind of wound up today."

"What else is new? Tedi, tell us more about this dating for jewelry thing," Chloe said eagerly.

"Maybe Travis will give you a bracelet made out of used dirt-bike parts," Riley teased her sister.

"Very funny," Chloe said. A blush crept into her cheeks.

Travis Morgan was a boy. Correction: a serious hottie Chloe was crushing on. A junior at West Malibu High, his great passion in life was his dirt bike, although Chloe was forever plotting to change that.

Mrs. Carlson hung up the phone. "Guess what? Maria Rodriguez wants to interview your dad and me here at the house, about the business! You know, for an article about couples working together—that kind of thing."

Riley was confused. Couples working together? "But Mom, you and Dad aren't, um, exactly a couple these days. And you don't work together anymore," she pointed out.

"I know, I know," Mrs. Carlson said, waving her hands. "But a life-style feature in the *Herald*—how could I pass that up? It'll be major publicity for the business. I just have to convince your father...." She picked up the phone and began dialing. "Come on, Jake, be home," she murmured to herself.

After their separation, Jake Carlson had decided to simplify his life. He lived in a small trailer overlooking the ocean. It was the same trailer park where Travis's family lived.

Jake was taking some time off, living on his savings and investments. Mostly, he spent his days doing yoga and meditation.

[<u>Riley</u>: **In other words, sitting and breathing deeply a lot.**]

"Darn, I got his machine," Mrs. Carlson said. "Jake? It's Macy. Listen, I need a favor. This can be a win-win for both of us. All I need you to do is to be here this Wednesday and talk to the *Herald* with me for forty-five minutes, an hour tops...."

Mrs. Carlson continued speed-talking into the phone and punching things into her Palm Pilot at the same time.

"Well, I'm off to make the zucchini waffles,"

Manuelo said, and he disappeared into the kitchen.

"I think I'll watch Manuelo," Chloe said, standing. "Since I'm going to be taking a cooking class, I guess I should be open to new food experiences. Maybe I can help him broil some water or something."

Riley tried not to laugh. "B*roil*?" she repeated. "Chloe, you don't broil water, you *boil* it!"

Chloe shrugged. "Broil…boil…whatever, Riley. It's only one letter different," she said, and headed into the kitchen.

Riley shook her head and laughed. Chloe had a lot to learn about cooking. Riley, on the other hand, knew that sewing was going to be a cinch. It was a brilliant choice for an elective.

After all, weren't both of her parents fashion designers? Weren't she and her sister clothing connoisseurs? So, how hard could stitching a few pieces of fabric together be?

This class will be an easy A, for sure.

chapter
two

Riley had only a few minutes to touch up her lip gloss before first period, Monday morning. She rushed into the girls' bathroom in the main hall of West Malibu High.

Joelle Myers, Carrie Thompson, and Tara Jordan were at the mirrors, touching up their makeup, too. "Hey, Riley," Joelle called over her shoulder.

"Hey, guys," Riley said. She hurried to a mirror, dug through her backpack, and pulled out a small pot of Very Berry. It went great with her red tank top and jeans. As she smoothed it over her lips, she murmured, "Sierra been here yet?"

"In here, Rile!" Sierra hopped out of one of the stalls as she slipped a pair of platform boots onto her feet. Her auburn hair flowed wildly around her shoulders. She was wearing tight, faded jeans and a glittery T-shirt that said *Rock Star*, and she was shoving a long pleated skirt into her backpack.

"You'll never believe this one," Sierra said. "My mom wants me to quit practicing the guitar. She was all, 'It's hardly a real instrument. You need to focus on the violin.' Can you believe that? I mean, if she only knew that my guitar and my band are my life!"

"If she only knew you were *in* a band, period," Riley said with a shrug.

Sierra laughed. "Right."

To Sierra's old-fashioned parents, Sierra was a quiet girl named Sarah, who played first violin in the school orchestra. They had no clue that their "Sarah" told everybody else to call her Sierra. That Sierra played bass guitar in a rock band called The Wave. That every morning their daughter rushed to the girls' room and changed out of the conservative "Sarah" clothes they picked out for her, and changed into one of the cool "Sierra" outfits she kept in her locker.

Riley got dizzy just thinking about what Sierra went through every day. Two identities. Riley had enough trouble dealing with one!

Riley checked her watch. "Got to go to my locker before sewing," she said, stuffing her lip gloss back into her backpack. "I'll see you in class, Sierra. Okay?"

"Yup," Sierra said, heading to the mirror to check her makeup.

"Bye, guys," Riley called to the girls in the bathroom. Then she rushed back into the hall—and ran smack into Alex Zimmer.

[Riley: Aggghhh! It's him. Ohmigosh. He's the lead guitarist in Sierra's band. Ever since he sang that song for me at the party Chloe and I had last week, I've been thinking about him. He is so cute...and so sweet...and...and...and he's staring as if he's waiting for me to say something. Ohmigosh!]

Alex spoke first. "Hey."

"Hey," Riley said, managing a smile.

Alex brushed his sandy-brown hair out of his eyes and smiled back. "How's it going?"

"Good," Riley replied. Good? That's really brilliant, Riley, she scolded herself.

"What class do you have next?" Alex asked her.

"Intro to sewing," Riley said. "I needed a new elective, and I thought that might be fun. You know, so I can learn to...sew stuff."

"Cool." Alex adjusted his backpack on his shoulder. His dark brown eyes stared into hers. "Listen. Maybe you'll be busy or whatever, but if you're not, do you want to..."

[Riley: Ohmigosh!]

"...get together after school or something?"

"YES!"

Riley was afraid she'd said that way too quickly and eagerly. But Alex didn't seem bothered in the least. In fact, he looked really happy.

13

"Cool. I'll see you then." He gave her a little wave and walked toward the science wing.

[Riley: Did you see that? Alex just asked me out. He asked me out! Meeeee!]

Riley could hardly contain herself. She took a deep breath and let it out in a big whoosh. Her heart was pounding like mad.

The bell rang, and she rushed to her locker, put away her heavy algebra book, then ran all the way to Room 112, Intro to Sewing.

Sierra was standing at one of the sewing-machine work stations. She waved Riley over.

"Hey!" Sierra called out. "What's up? You look way happier than you did in the girls' room. Like you just scored free passes to the Raging Dogs concert or something."

Riley squeezed Sierra's arm. "Guess what? Alex asked me out!"

Sierra gasped. "Oh, wow, that is so great!"

"We're getting together after school. I am totally psyched!" Riley cried.

"Did he mention our new gig?" Sierra asked.

Riley shook her head. "No. What gig?"

"We're playing at California Dream again this Saturday," Sierra said excitedly. California Dream was a local beach club and hangout. The Wave had played there for the first time several weeks ago.

"Wow, congratulations." Riley and Sierra exchanged high fives.

Just then, Larry Slotnick strolled into class. Riley's smile faded a little. Larry was the Carlsons' goofy next-door neighbor. He had spiky brown hair, close-together eyes, a big mouth that was always sporting a silly grin, and an eternal crush on Riley.

"Greetings!" Larry called out. "Is this seat taken? No?" He pulled up a chair next to Riley. "See, Riley? Fate always brings us together."

More like bad luck, Riley thought. "Um, what are you doing here, Larry?" Riley asked.

"I'm taking sewing, same as yourself," Larry replied.

"I didn't know you were into sewing," Riley said.

Larry batted his eyelashes. "I'd do anything to be near you, Riley." He sighed.

[Riley: Okay. It's not that I don't think Larry's a great guy. He's sweet, he's loyal, he's dependable—a really good friend. It's just that in his mind, he and I are riding off into the sunset together. And I don't feel "that way" about him. Now, Alex, he's a different story. He's definitely sunset material....]

A short blond woman walked to the front of the class. She rapped a pair of knitting needles against the blackboard to get the students' attention. Riley knew she was the sewing teacher, Ms. Spoke.

15

"Good morning, ladies—and Larry," Ms. Spoke said. "Today, we're going to make aprons."

Riley glanced around the room. She realized that Larry was the only boy in the class.

"Okay, class," Ms. Spoke said. "First you need to pick out the fabric and pattern you want to use. Then take your apron patterns and pin them onto the fabric, like this, and cut them out." She demonstrated on a piece of fabric that had puppies and kittens all over it.

Riley went to the front of the room, where dozens of fabrics lay on a long table. She grabbed a piece of simple white cotton material and a box of straight pins. Then she picked out a pattern labeled Basic Apron.

Basic. That sounds pretty easy, she thought.

Back at her workstation, Riley unfolded the apron pattern—a piece of thin paper with marks and lines all over it. She began pinning it to the white material.

"Ow!" Riley cried, sticking herself with a pin. She sucked on her finger for a second, then began again.

As she worked, she watched Larry out of the corner of her eye. Larry sure seems to know what he's doing, Riley thought. He finished pinning his apron in about five minutes.

Where did Larry learn to do that? she wondered. She stopped pinning and stared at him in fascination.

"Earth to Riley," Larry said. "What's up? Why aren't you pinning? Pins are our friends!"

"I'm pinning, I'm pinning," Riley grumbled.

Sierra had finished pinning, too. She proceeded to cut two pieces of denim into what looked like thick lightning bolts. She held them up. "Pockets," she said, nodding approvingly.

"When you're done pinning and cutting around your pattern, you may begin sewing," Ms. Spoke announced. "If anyone needs help, just raise your hand."

The room soon filled with the whirring sound of sewing machines. Riley finally finished pinning and cutting. Her fabric didn't exactly look apron-shaped, though. More like a bunch of big zigzaggy bandannas. Maybe it will look more apronlike after the sewing part, she told herself.

Okay. Now I just have to get this sewing machine going, Riley thought. She took two white zigzaggy fabric squares and scooted them under the needle. She sat there and stared at the machine.

Larry leaned over. "What's up? Why aren't you sewing away?"

"I just remembered that I've never used one of these things in my life," Riley admitted.

"But your mom and dad are fashion designers. You've been around sewing machines since you were a baby," Sierra piped up.

"Yeah. And all I can remember is Mom and Dad saying, 'No! Careful! Don't touch!'" Riley said, imitating her parents.

Larry patted her shoulder. "Relax. It's not going to

hurt you. Here, let me show you how." He quickly threaded her machine and repositioned the white cotton for her.

"Hey, sewing boy, you forgot your purse!"

Riley glanced up and turned around. Two burly guys—Bob something and Juan something from the football team—were peering in through the doorway. Juan grabbed a small wicker sewing basket that was sitting on the counter and tossed it at Larry.

Larry caught it and tried to whip it back at the boys. It didn't reach them, and landed in the center of the classroom.

"Great arm, Slotnick," Bob said. He and Juan laughed hysterically.

"Why aren't you two gentlemen in class?" Ms. Spoke demanded, striding quickly toward the door.

Larry and Riley turned back to their machines.

"I'm never going to live this down," Larry said. "They'll torture me all year."

"You've got to stand up for yourself, Larry," Riley replied.

"Yeah, right," Larry said, "and then Bob and Juan would cream me!"

Riley didn't know what to say next, so she switched on her sewing machine. "Well, I'm going to nail this apron thing."

The sewing machine whirred to life. Riley directed the white cotton fabric under the needle, the same way she had seen her parents do hundreds of times at home.

But instead of nice, neat stitches that went in a straight line, Riley's stitches went all over the place. After a minute, she stopped the machine and eased the fabric out.

Her creation was all bunched up, like a wadded dish towel. It didn't look anything like an apron.

[<u>Riley</u>: I know. This should be easy, right? You cut the fabric. You sew the fabric, right? So why can't I seem to do this? Where are those sewing genes when I need them?]

Riley wanted to whine to Sierra about it, but her friend had gone across the room to search for some cool-looking fabric scraps.

"Done!" Larry announced, shutting off his machine.

Riley sighed. "Let me see."

Larry slipped his apron over Riley's head. It was orange and pink, with an oven mitt secured to each side.

"Larry, this is really good!" Riley said, surprised. "I had no idea you were so talented."

"Me, either," Larry said with a grin.

Ms. Spoke walked by and glanced at the orange-and-pink apron. "Riley!" she exclaimed. "Your apron is wonderful. An A plus!"

Riley shook her head quickly. Ms. Spoke had the wrong idea! "No, you don't understand. This—"

"Congratulations, Riley!" Larry said, slapping her on

the back. "Isn't she talented, Ms. Spoke? Aren't we just so proud of her?"

"Absolutely," Ms. Spoke replied.

"But…" Riley said. She didn't want to take credit for something she didn't do. It was Larry's apron, not hers!

Ms. Spoke moved on. Riley leaned toward Larry. "I can't take credit for your apron," she whispered. "It would be wrong for me to get an A plus I didn't earn. It would be *great*, but it would be wrong."

"Come on, Riley. Do me a favor," Larry said in a low voice. "It's embarrassing enough to be in sewing class. It would be humiliating if Bob and Juan found out I was actually good at it." He added, "Please, Riley, I'm begging you. Take my A plus. Just this once."

Riley sighed. She had a bad feeling about it in the pit of her stomach. She opened her mouth to say "No way," but instead she blurted out, "Oh, all right."

I am *so* going to regret this, Riley thought as Larry grinned and slapped her back again.

chapter
three

Room 120 was filled with the yummy smell of chocolate. This is going to be fun, Chloe thought, tying on a white apron over her denim skirt and pink T-shirt.

"Our assignment today is brownies," Mr. Ferguson, the cooking teacher, announced. He wore khakis, a button-down shirt that was a bit too snug in the stomach area, and a tie with little vegetable designs all over it. A tall white chef's hat covered his short black hair.

"I've written out the recipe on the blackboard, and you will find the ingredients at your workstations," Mr. Ferguson went on. "I will be going around the room to check on your progress. The ovens have been set to three-fifty, so they're ready to go."

Three-fifty? Chloe wondered. She glanced at her watch. It's only ten in the morning. Does that mean the brownies have to cook for six hours?

"I love brownies," Amanda whispered to Chloe.

"Me, too," Chloe replied. She was really glad she had decided to take cooking with Amanda.

Appearance- and personality-wise, Amanda Gray kind of matched her last name. She dressed plainly, in a way that made people not notice her. She was kind of shy and didn't socialize much.

On the other hand, in the short time Chloe had known her, she'd discovered another Amanda. Despite her mousy appearance and shy demeanor, Amanda was confident, fun, funny, and supersmart. She was a great person to hang out with.

"Okay, let's get this operation going," Chloe told Amanda. "Bowl, mixing spoon, baking pan..." She mentally checked off each item. She had everything she needed in front of her.

Amanda grabbed her measuring cup and dumped some flour into it, disregarding the measurement lines on the cup. "I'm really good at eyeballing."

"Eyeballing?" Chloe repeated. "Sounds gruesome."

Amanda laughed. "It means you just look at the amount without really measuring it. If you cook a lot, you get really good at eyeballing."

Chloe picked up her own measuring cup and a bag of flour. Okay, I'll try this eyeballing thing, too, she thought, ignoring the numbers and lines on the measuring cup.

She tilted the bag over the cup, but the flour poured out too fast and cascaded all over the counter. Chloe coughed and tried to brush away the flour. But soon, her pink T-shirt, denim skirt, and apron were covered with white.

[Chloe: A little bit of advice: Wear all white the next time you try to bake.]

"I make brownies all the time at home, with my mom," Amanda told Chloe as she worked. "We change the basic recipe around and add different ingredients to it. We've made white chocolate brownies, butterscotch brownies, macadamia nut brownies with coconut frosting...."

"You can do that?" Chloe asked her. "Change the recipe?"

"Sure!" Amanda said. "You can do whatever you want."

As Amanda talked, she cut a small chunk of butter with a knife. Chloe did the same. But the butter skidded across the counter and fell to the floor. She picked it up and put it back on the counter. It was gooey and covered with flour and dirt.

Chloe grimaced, wiping her greasy hands on her apron. She thought about what Amanda had just said. Changing the recipe. It was an intriguing idea.

On an impulse, she walked over to the massive steel refrigerator in the corner and opened it. The shelves were loaded with vegetables, fruits, milk, and various jars of stuff.

She saw a jar way in the back of the refrigerator, labeled *Truffle butter*.

Truffles. Those are really, really fancy chocolates, Chloe remembered. One of her mom's clients sent her a box of truffles once. Chloe and Riley went through them in a couple of days.

[Chloe: Okay, maybe more like a couple of hours.]

Maybe she should replace the regular butter in her brownies with this truffle butter stuff—to make them extra-special and chocolatey, Chloe thought excitedly. Then Mr. Ferguson would be really impressed and give her an A.

She headed back to her workstation with the jar. Amanda was pouring her brownie batter into a square baking pan.

"You're done already?" Chloe said.

"Yup. It's all ready to bake," Amanda replied. She headed over to one of the ovens.

Chloe brushed a lock of wavy blond hair off her forehead. She'd better get busy. She read Mr. Ferguson's recipe on the board. Step Four: Cream eggs, butter and chocolate. What was she supposed to do with the cream, eggs, butter and chocolate? And what did the next step mean? Gradually fold flour mix into wet mix. How could you fold flour?

She glanced around, looking for Amanda, but Amanda was busy dealing with her own brownies at one of the ovens. Then Chloe looked around for Mr.

Ferguson. He was occupied, too, helping out some other students across the room.

> [Chloe: So maybe this cooking business is more complicated than I thought. I know I can do this, though. I've watched Manuelo in the kitchen day after day. Most of the time, he doesn't even use a cookbook. He just throws in a dash of this, a pinch of that, and voila! Magic! Except maybe those zucchini waffles.]

So, no problem, I can do this on my own, Chloe thought. She eyeballed the eggs, flour, sugar, and chocolate, pouring them into a bowl. Then she added the truffle butter, and mixed the ingredients together.

It looks pretty gross, Chloe thought. But, hey, it's going to look even worse once it's in my stomach, right?

Soon, Chloe poured her mixture into a pan. She was the last one to put her pan into the oven. By the time all the brownies were done, it was almost the end of class. Mr. Ferguson went around the room, sampling everyone's work.

Amanda's brownies looked perfect. "Now, *these* are brownies!" Mr. Ferguson exclaimed, tasting a sample. "You get an A plus!"

Amanda beamed. "Wow! Thank you, Mr. Ferguson!"

Mr. Ferguson reached for Chloe's pan next. "What is this?" he asked. "Molten lava?" He wrinkled his nose. "Are you sure these are done, Ms. Carlson?"

"I'm totally sure," Chloe said cheerfully. "Try one!"

Mr. Ferguson dipped his finger into the pan and tasted Chloe's brownie. He coughed. "Uh, w-what did you put in these?" he sputtered.

"Everything you wrote on the board," Chloe replied. "Plus my special secret ingredient. Truffle butter!"

"Truffle butter! You put mushrooms in your brownies?" Mr. Ferguson gasped.

"Mushrooms? I thought truffles were chocolates," Chloe said, confused.

"There *are* chocolate truffles," Mr. Ferguson said. "They're candies. But real truffles are a rare type of mushroom," he explained, frowning. "I had that truffle butter in the refrigerator from a special demonstration I gave last week. It's extremely expensive."

Chloe winced. "Oh. Sorry!"

Mr. Ferguson shook his head and went on to the next student.

A few minutes later, the bell rang. Amanda and Chloe scrambled to clean up.

"Better luck next time," Amanda said to Chloe. "Hey, maybe you could come over after school sometime and make brownies with my mom and me."

Chloe sighed. "Sure. Just keep me away from the mushrooms," she said.

Just then, Travis Morgan popped his head into the room. He sidled over to Chloe and Amanda. "Hey, Chloe," he said, giving her the most adorable lopsided smile.

Chloe's heart did a somersault. Travis! Walking into her classroom! Was it her imagination, or did he look even cuter than the last time she saw him? He was wearing denim jeans and a T-shirt that complemented his short, sun-bleached brown hair. Sunlight slanting through the window lit up the tiny gold piercing in his ear.

He reached over and brushed something off her cheek. "Flour," he murmured.

Chloe blushed. "Oh. Thanks." She had a brief mental image of drawing a heart on her cheek with an eyebrow pencil and writing in the center, Travis Was Here.

Come on, Chloe. Make conversation, she told herself. "So, um, how's it going, Travis?"

"Great. I smelled brownies and thought I'd try to score some," he said. "My next class is Alge-*bore*, so I figured I'd need the energy."

"Oh, definitely," Chloe agreed.

Travis eyed Chloe's pan of brownies. "Gross. What is that?" he said, grimacing. "Dude, I wouldn't eat that if you paid me!"

Chloe was about to say, "Those are brownies in progress." But before she had a chance, Travis reached for one of Amanda's brownies.

"Mmm," he said, chewing enthusiastically. "Chloe, awesome brownie. You're an excellent cook."

"But…" Chloe began.

She glanced over at Amanda. Her friend was busy talking to Joelle.

"Can I have another one for the road?" Travis asked.

"Uh, you sure you don't want to try one of these?" Chloe held up her pan.

"You're funny, Chloe." Travis laughed. "I feel sorry for the person who has to eat those!"

He grabbed another brownie from Amanda's pan and popped it into his mouth. "Well, see you!" he mumbled, his mouth full of brownie.

Amanda's brownie, Chloe thought. "Uh, sure. See you."

[Chloe: What? Why are you looking at me like that? So what if I accidentally forgot to mention to Travis that he was eating Amanda's brownies, not mine? I mean, what's the harm in having a really hot guy think you're an excellent cook? It's no big deal, right?]

chapter
four

"This ice cream is awesome," Riley said to Alex as they strolled along the beach after school. They'd stopped at an ice cream shop earlier, where Alex bought them each a cone.

"Chocolate Raspberry Ripple. It's great, isn't it? It's one of my favorites," Alex said.

Riley felt the cool sand between her bare toes. She tried to focus on what Alex was saying, but her heart was hammering in her chest. She couldn't remember the last time she felt so nervous—or happy.

"So like I was saying before, my mom is a pediatrician," Alex said. "And my dad's a lawyer, although he used to play guitar in high school. Just like me."

"Do you have any brothers or sisters?" Riley asked.

"I have a little brother, Zach. He's six. I help take care of him a lot, since my mom and dad have such crazy work schedules," Alex replied.

"I know what that's like," Riley said, nodding. "My mom is a fashion designer. She and my dad used to run the business together, but now they're separated, so she does it all herself. She's pretty nuts all the time."

"That must be tough," Alex said, "your parents being separated and all."

Riley smiled at him. He was so nice. Nice…and cute. "It was weird at first," she said after a minute. "But they seem to be getting along better, now that they're not living together. If that makes any sense."

"Sure, that makes sense." Alex smiled and moved closer to her. The next thing she knew, Alex took her hand and squeezed it.

Riley almost dropped her Chocolate Raspberry Ripple into the sand. First they were on a date, and now Alex was holding her hand. This was so unbelievably awesome!

"Um, your band," Riley squeaked. She tried to get her voice under control. "Your band," she repeated. "Sierra told me you guys are playing at California Dream again this weekend." His fingers felt so warm and wonderful intertwined with hers.

"Yeah," Alex said, taking a bite of his cone. "I'm pretty psyched about that. You're coming, aren't you?" he added eagerly. "Maybe we could hang out after the show."

Riley nodded yes, yes, yes. "I wouldn't miss it."

"Great," Alex said.

A wave rolled in, tickled her feet, then receded. The sun glittered on the blue water. Everything was so perfect: the sun…the waves…the palm trees swaying in the breeze…Alex. Riley didn't want their date to end.

The beach was deserted. Except for one lone girl jogging toward them. As she neared, Riley noticed that the girl was tall and slender, with a long platinum-blond ponytail.

Alex noticed her, too—and he suddenly dropped Riley's hand.

"Alex!" the girl cried out. She jogged up to him and gave him a big, sweaty hug.

[Riley: Okay, who is this person? Why is she hugging Alex? Why is he hugging her? Why don't they stop hugging, already?]

After what seemed to be hours, the girl untangled her sweaty, perfect body from Alex and beamed at him. "How are you? It's been ages." She squeezed his arm.

"Um, yeah," Alex said. He sounded flustered.

He turned to Riley. "Willow, this is Riley Carlson. Riley, this is Willow Sweet. She's…an old friend of mine."

[Riley: "Old friend"? Do old friends hug like that? I don't think so.]

Willow smiled at Riley. "Hey, it's so nice to meet you! Do you go to West Malibu High, too?"

"Uh-huh," Riley replied. She couldn't stop staring at Willow. She'd never seen anyone so totally pretty before. Willow was even more gorgeous than Tedi.

"And where do you go to school?" Riley managed to ask after a minute. Say you're visiting from somewhere else, she prayed. Like Australia.

"My family just moved back to Malibu," Willow explained. "We moved away for a while...but now we're back." She reached out and squeezed Alex's arm again.

"You're going to West Malibu High?" Alex asked her, surprised.

Riley noticed that Willow still had her hand on Alex's arm—and that Alex wasn't moving it away. She frowned.

Willow nodded. "Isn't that great? I start classes tomorrow."

Willow said something else to Alex—something about her parents—but Riley barely heard her. Her mind was racing.

Willow seemed supernice. She also seemed super-touchy-feely with Alex. Was it Riley's imagination, or were the two of them definitely more than just "old friends"?

"Riley?"

Riley's head shot up. Alex was staring at her.

"Huh?" Riley said.

"Willow was wondering if you and I could give her some advice about teachers," Alex said. "Like that sewing teacher—don't you have her? Plus some of the other ones."

"Sure, anytime," Riley said to Willow. "No problem."

"Great! That is so sweet of you. Well, better get back to my jog. See you guys later!" Willow gave a little wave and began running up the beach again.

Riley and Alex resumed their walk. Riley suddenly realized that her ice cream had melted. Her cone was now a sorry-looking, soggy lump—kind of like how she felt inside.

Alex didn't say a word. He didn't take her hand again, either. He just stared ahead at the horizon.

"Soooo," Riley said after a moment. "Willow seems nice."

"Yeah." Alex turned to her abruptly. "Look, I should tell you."

Riley's heart lurched in her chest. "Tell me what?"

"Willow and I used to go out," Alex confessed. "But it was over a long time ago. I just want you to know that."

"Oh, don't worry about it," Riley said, forcing herself to smile. "I totally understand. It's not a problem."

But inside she was thinking, Willow looks like Gwyneth Paltrow. She's even nice. Why was Alex crazy enough to stop dating her? And what's going to stop him from taking up where he left off?

chapter five

"**O**w!" That was the second nail Chloe broke on the can opener. This cooking thing sure is a pain, she thought in annoyance.

Chloe pulled her emergency emery board out of her jeans pocket and filed down the broken nail. She was working on tomorrow's cooking-class assignment: Make Your Favorite Dish. Her favorite dish happened to be Manuelo's beef stroganoff. She'd found the recipe for it on the family computer.

She had watched Manuelo put it together a hundred times. He always made it look so easy. So why was she having such a hard time? This was her third try—no, fourth—and they were all terrible. The last one *looked* the closest to Manuelo's stroganoff, but it still tasted pretty disgusting.

Plus, she was ruining her manicure.

Plus, the kitchen was a total mess. Dirty pots and

pans were piled everywhere, and stroganoff sauce dotted the floor, walls, and ceiling.

The late-afternoon sun slanted through the window. Pepper lay on the floor, thumping her tail, drifting in and out of sleep. "You're no help," Chloe said to the dog.

Pepper opened one eye, thumped her tail, then went back to sleep.

Chloe stirred her latest pot of stroganoff, which was bubbling away on the stove. She lifted the spatula to her lips, tasted it, and grimaced. Yup, it was still terrible.

The phone rang. Chloe stepped over some dirty bowls on the floor and grabbed the phone. "Hello?"

Chloe could hear a song playing on the other end, then, "Hey, Chloe, it's me."

Chloe recognized the voice. "Hey, Amanda, what's up?"

"Not much. What're you doing?"

"Oh, just, you know, cooking up a storm for tomorrow's class," Chloe said. *Storm* was right, she thought, glancing around the kitchen. "I can't quite seem to nail this beef stroganoff recipe."

Just then, Chloe heard a beep on the phone. "Call waiting," she announced to Amanda. "Hang on."

Chloe pressed a button. "Hello?" she said to the second caller.

"Hey. Chloe?"

That voice. She knew instantly who it was. "Yes, this is Chloe," she said breathlessly.

"It's Travis."

35

Chloe cheered silently. Calm down, she told herself. "Um, hey, Travis, how's it going?" she said.

"Not bad. Listen. I was wondering if you wanted to grab a slice of pizza."

Chloe pumped a fist in the air and mouthed the word *yes*! Unfortunately, she forgot that she was holding a drippy spatula, and brown stroganoff sauce splattered all over the floor. "Oops!"

"What did you say?" Travis asked her.

"I said, 'Pizza? You mean right now?'" Chloe improvised quickly.

"Uh-huh," Travis said.

Chloe was about to tell him that she'd be there in ten seconds. A date with Travis—finally! She'd been dreaming about this ever since the first day of school!

But before she said yes, she scanned the kitchen. She saw about twenty dirty pots and pans. Plus, stroganoff sauce now adorned just about every surface.

Could she clean up really fast, then go and meet Travis? she wondered.

As she was considering this, the flame under the pot with the stroganoff started hissing and spitting. Her dish towel, which she had left near the pot, caught fire and started burning.

"Chloe? How about that pizza?" Travis was saying on the other end of the phone.

"Sorry, maybe another time! Kitchen fire! Gotta go!" Chloe shouted.

She slammed down the phone and picked up the fire extinguisher that Manuelo kept near the stove. Within seconds, the fire was out.

"Oh, boy," Chloe said, slumping against the counter. Now, she was covered with stroganoff sauce *and* white foam.

At this rate, I'll never get a good grade in cooking, she thought. And then she remembered that she'd left Amanda on hold. She'd better call her back and explain.

The kitchen door opened, and Riley walked in. She slipped her backpack off her shoulder and dropped it on a chair. "Hey," she called out in a glum-sounding voice.

"Hey!" Chloe said. "Didn't you have a date with Alex? How'd it go? Tell me everything!"

"Not now," Riley muttered. "Bad mood."

"Uh-oh." Chloe could tell her sister didn't want to talk about it. Maybe later, she thought.

Chloe glanced around. "I'd offer you some sympathy cookies, but I'm not sure I could find any. The kitchen's kind of a disaster right now."

"Yeah, I noticed," Riley said, sniffing the air. "Smells like a McDonald's burned down in here."

"Long story. Basic cooking isn't so basic. Hey, how did sewing class go today?" Chloe asked her sister, trying to change the subject.

"Not so well." Riley reached into her backpack and pulled out a pink and orange apron. "We had to make aprons in class—"

"And you made that one?" Chloe interrupted. She grabbed it from Riley and slipped it on over her head. "It's totally cool!"

"Yeah, except I didn't make it. Larry did. But there was a misunderstanding, and Ms. Spoke thought I made it. So she kind of gave me an A plus," Riley admitted.

Chloe clucked her tongue. "You be careful, girl. You might get into serious trouble if she finds out about it."

"I know, I know," Riley said. "Don't remind me."

Riley took off upstairs to do some homework, and Chloe called Amanda to apologize for hanging up on her.

Then she turned back to the messy kitchen, wondering where to start. She had to clean before Manuelo got home from the store.

Too late. Manuelo burst through the kitchen door, his arms filled with grocery bags. "You wouldn't believe the avocados at the market today!" he said happily. Then he took a look at the mess in the kitchen and gasped. "Oh, my goodness! What happened here?"

Chloe smiled apologetically. "I was, um, trying to make your beef stroganoff."

"Why? If you wanted my stroganoff, all you had to do was ask!" Manuelo cried out.

He set the grocery bags on the counter and rushed to the refrigerator. He opened the freezer and pulled out a plastic bag filled with something brown.

"Manuelo's Meal in a Minute!" he announced, holding up the Baggie. "Pop it in the microwave and, presto—Manuelo's genuine Russian-Rican stroganoff! I keep dozens of them in here. See? No need to start fires," he said.

Chloe shook her head. "I don't want to eat it. I want to make it. For school tomorrow. I'm supposed to whip up my favorite meal for cooking class."

"Stroganoff is not so easy," Manuelo warned her, putting the bag back in the freezer. "Maybe you should try something simple. Like toast."

"I can't get a good grade with toast," Chloe said, sighing. "Don't worry, Manuelo. I'll figure out something."

Manuelo shrugged. "Okey-dokey." He put away the groceries and left the kitchen.

Alone again, Chloe leaned against the counter. Her gaze moved from the stroganoff-spattered floor to the refrigerator to the freezer door. All of a sudden, she had a very bad, very brilliant thought.

What if? she thought. It would be just this one time....

Chloe shook her head quickly. She was ashamed of even thinking about it. How could she use one of Manuelo's Meals in a Minute for her cooking class? It would be cheating!

But the next thing she knew, she was walking toward the refrigerator, opening the freezer door, and taking out one of Manuelo's bags.

● ● ●

Riley was supposed to be doing her American history homework. Except she could hardly concentrate on American history. All she could think about was Alex's history—specifically, his history with the infuriatingly perfect Willow.

On one of the blank pages in her notebook, she had written:

> The Declaration of Independence was
> adopted in 1776.
> Alex + Willow?
> Alex + Me?

She picked up a purple Magic Marker and scratched out those words. Then she ripped out the piece of paper from her notebook, crumpled it into a ball, and attempted a three-point shot into the wastebasket across the room. She missed.

There was a knock on the door.

"What?" Riley snapped.

"Honey?"

The door creaked opened, and Mrs. Carlson walked in—followed by Mr. Carlson. Jake Carlson was dressed in shorts, flip-flops, and a T-shirt that said BE HERE NOW. A baseball cap covered his brown hair, and his eyes sparkled behind a pair of horn-rimmed glasses.

"Dad? What are you doing here?" Riley asked, surprised. She stood up and gave him a big hug.

"Your mom asked me to come over to discuss the

Herald interview," Mr. Carlson explained, hugging her back.

"We ran into Chloe in the kitchen," Mrs. Carlson cut in. "We noticed her fabulous apron right away—well, after we noticed that huge mess. Anyway, we asked her where she got it. She said that *you* brought it from your sewing class, sweetie!"

"And that you got an A plus for it," Mr. Carlson added. "We are so proud of you, pumpkin!"

Riley gulped. For a brief second, she was furious at Chloe for passing on that little white lie. But then she realized there was no way she could have expected Chloe not to—especially if Chloe was caught off guard.

"Uh, thanks, Mom, Dad," Riley said. She hoped they would drop the topic. But they didn't.

"How did you come up with that design, anyway?" Mr. Carlson asked her.

"It's very innovative, very bold!" Mrs. Carlson agreed.

Where's Larry when you need him? Riley wondered. Out loud, she said, "Well, uh, I was just kind of, uh, doodling in my notebook, and there it was."

"That is so wonderful," Mrs. Carlson gushed. "Our little girl is a designer!"

"Hey!" Mr. Carlson exclaimed, sitting down on the edge of Riley's bed. "This gives me an idea. Why don't you share some of your designs with Maria Rodriguez during the Herald interview?"

"Huh?" Riley said.

"That's a great idea, Jake!" Mrs. Carlson said enthusiastically.

"But, Mom, I—" Riley began.

"I know what you're thinking," Mr. Carlson cut in. "They're just doodles. But that's how exciting designs are formed!"

[Riley: Not exactly what I was thinking. More like, how am I going to get myself out of this? Answer: I can't.]

"Well, if you don't want to show Maria Rodriguez your doodles, maybe you can sketch a couple of new things," Mom suggested. "Nothing too complicated, of course."

"Of course," Riley said as her stomach twisted itself into a tight knot. "No problem."

"Are you feeling okay, honey?" Mrs. Carlson asked her, looking concerned.

"Oh, sure, Mom. I feel great!" Riley faked a happy smile. "This is an awesome opportunity!" To make a fool of myself, she thought.

After her parents left, Riley sat at her desk. She immediately began scribbling on a blank piece of paper.

"I hope this drawing stuff is easier than sewing," she muttered to herself.

chapter
six

"**S**o, what did you make for today's assignment?" Amanda asked Chloe.

It was Tuesday morning, and Amanda and Chloe were in cooking class. Mr. Ferguson was walking around the room, tasting everyone's homework assignments and grading them on the spot.

Chloe removed the lid from her covered dish. The delicious aroma of beef wafted into the air. "Beef stroganoff," she mumbled.

"Wow, smells delicious," Amanda said. "I guess you got that recipe down, after all."

"Uh-huh," Chloe said uncomfortably. "I guess I did."

Amanda lifted a corner of aluminum foil from her pan. "I made a shrimp and papaya pizza. I hope Mr. Ferguson likes it."

"That looks awesome," Chloe complimented her.

Chloe felt a wave of guilt. Amanda was becoming a

real cook. Chloe merely took other people's frozen creations, defrosted them, and passed them off as her own.

Okay, stop it, Chloe told herself. It was an emergency. I needed the grade. Besides, Manuelo's never going to find out one of his Baggies is missing because I replaced it with a Baggie of *my* stroganoff.

Mr. Ferguson approached Chloe. "All right, Ms. Carlson, what have you made for us?" Before waiting for a reply, he took the lid off her dish. "Mmm, smells like beef stroganoff!"

"Uh-huh," Chloe said.

"What kind of paprika did you use?" Mr. Ferguson asked. "Was it Hungarian, or—"

"Puerto Rican!" Chloe blurted out. "I used Puerto Rican paprika."

Mr. Ferguson looked puzzled. "That must be a new variety. And what about the sour cream? Regular or nonfat? Or did you substitute yogurt?"

Chloe searched her brain. What did Manuelo use? "Sour cream," she guessed. "With fat."

Mr. Ferguson nodded. "Very good."

He dipped his fork into the beef stroganoff and took a bite. His face lit up. "Delicious! Fabulous! Ms. Carlson, I can honestly say this is one of the best stroganoffs I've ever tasted."

Another wave of guilt passed through Chloe. "Oh, great," she muttered. "I mean, oh, great!" she said loudly. "Thank you, Mr. Ferguson!"

"A plus," Mr. Ferguson said. "Class, I suggest you gather around and have a taste of Ms. Carlson's creation. It's truly exemplary."

"Wow, like, you're going to be the next Martha Stewart or whatever," Amanda complimented Chloe.

Chloe shrugged. "Or whatever."

"Class, we have another new student joining us," Ms. Spoke announced in sewing class that day.

Riley barely glanced up from her notebook. She was supposed to be working on today's assignment: a pair of curtains. What was up with that, anyway? she wondered. Couldn't you just buy some roll-down shades?

In any case, Riley was paying zero attention to the curtain-making project because she was too busy working on the sketches for tomorrow's *Herald* interview. She had her notebook half-hidden under the curtain fabric, so Ms. Spoke wouldn't notice.

"I don't believe it," Riley heard Sierra say. "Wow, she looks good."

"Riley is way more beautiful than her, in my humble opinion," Larry piped up from the other side.

Riley glanced up. Her breath caught in her throat. Willow Sweet was standing in the doorway with Ms. Spoke.

Willow looked even better without her sweaty running clothes and with makeup on. She was wearing a baby-blue T-shirt that complemented her slender frame and a short denim skirt that showed off her long, long, long legs. Her long superblond hair fell softly below her shoulders.

"Class, this is Willow Sweet," Ms. Spoke said. "Willow, why don't you sit…" She paused and glanced around, then pointed. "…over there? To the right of Larry Slotnick."

"Okay," Willow said. She sauntered to Larry's workstation and pulled up a chair. "Hi," she said to Larry. "I'm Willow." Then she noticed Riley, and her brown eyes lit up. "Hey, Riley! I forgot that Alex mentioned you were in this class. Wow, this is so awesome."

"You two know each other?" Larry asked, glancing back and forth.

"Yeah, we met yesterday," Riley said.

"Hey, Willow, welcome back," Sierra called to her.

"Oh, wow, hey, Sierra! It is so great to see you! Alex told me you two were in a band together," Willow said.

Alex told me. Those words stuck in Riley's brain. Ever since yesterday afternoon on the beach, Riley couldn't stop thinking about Willow and Alex together…as a couple.

Why was it bothering her so much? Didn't she and Alex have another date this afternoon?

Riley and Alex. Not Willow and Alex.

Riley checked the clock. Thirty minutes till the end of class. While the other students worked on their curtains, she turned her attention back to her sketches.

46

They weren't going so well. In fact, they weren't going, period.

"So Bob and Juan were totally ragging on me this morning about being in this class," Larry complained to Riley as he hand-stitched a hem. "What is their problem, anyway? I mean, haven't they ever heard of Calvin Klein?" He stopped. "Hey, Riley, I'm pouring my heart out to you, are you listening?"

"Huh?" Riley said, glancing up from her sketches.

"What are you doing, anyway?" Larry asked her.

Riley sighed and told him about the sketches she had to do for tomorrow's *Malibu Herald* interview.

Larry looked interested. He grabbed her notebook out of her hands and gazed at Riley's sketches. "Here, why don't you try something like this?" he said, scribbling over one of the drawings. Within seconds, he had transformed her incoherent squiggles into a cool-looking design for a dress. "In fact, this fabric we're using for the curtains might work. Check this out."

He picked up the curtain he was working on and draped it over his body. Tucking in a corner here and a corner there, the curtain almost looked like a dress. Riley had to admit, Larry seemed to know what he was doing.

"See how this line flatters the shoulders?" Larry said. "See how slimming it is through the waist? See how—"

"Yo, Slotnick, you look so hot in your new dress!

Will you go to the prom with me?" Bob the football player was standing in the doorway. He was pointing at Larry and laughing loudly.

"Hey, Bob, get a life," Riley snapped before she knew what she was saying. "And get a brain while you're at it! This is a toga, not a dress. Are you totally ignorant or what?"

Bob glared at her and walked off.

Larry smiled weakly at her. "You're good," he said.

"So are you," Riley said, nodding at Larry's dress. "I wish I could design half as well as you do."

Larry looked as though he was thinking something. "Hey, I'll make you a deal. I'll draw your sketches for you in time for that *Herald* interview. In exchange, you get Bob and Juan and those other jocks off my back about being in this class."

Riley didn't answer. On the one hand, she didn't want to lie to her parents—or to the reporter, Maria Rodriguez.

On the other hand, she didn't want to embarrass her parents with her lame sketches tomorrow night.

"Come on," Larry insisted. "This is a perfect plan. It can't go wrong."

"Oh, okay," she said finally. "I guess it's a deal."

Larry grinned. "Great. Since we're in a yes mood, will you go out with me?"

"No!" Riley laughed. "Now get back to work."

"Okay, okay," Larry said.

Riley looked at her notebook. Maybe this deal wasn't such a bad idea, after all. Larry was sure to produce some awesome sketches in time for tomorrow night's interview.

Of course, that also meant she would have to figure out a way to get Bob and Juan off Larry's back. But how hard could it be? she told herself.

"Riley?" Larry asked.

She glanced up. Larry had rewrapped her curtain fabric around him so that it was puffing out at the sides. "Does this make me look fat?"

Riley sighed. On second thought, it could be really tough, she decided.

chapter
seven

After school, Riley headed straight for the girls' bathroom. She brushed her hair until it was supershiny.

She and Alex were going to a new pizza place near the school. Then they'd go Rollerblading on the boardwalk.

And I won't worry about Willow, Riley told herself. I'll just focus on Alex and have fun.

Sierra rushed in. "Hey, Riley," she called out breathlessly. "Alex was looking for you. He gave me this note."

Sierra handed her a folded-up piece of paper. Riley unfolded and read it:

Riley,
I totally forgot that we have band practice after school. Can we try for another time? I'm really sorry.
                                        Alex

Riley reread the note. Her heart sank. She was really looking forward to this date.

Sierra was putting her hair up in a ponytail. "What's up? You look like your best friend died. Oops! I'm your best friend!"

Riley showed her the note. "We had a date. I guess we don't anymore," she said glumly.

"Oh." Sierra nodded. "Bummer." And then her expression brightened. "Listen, why don't you come to the practice? At least that way you can hang out with Alex and me and the rest of the band." She peeled off her tight jeans and pulled on a conservative skirt.

"That's a great idea," Riley said eagerly. She watched as Sierra slipped a baggy beige turtleneck over her scoop-necked T-shirt. "Uh, Sierra? Is that your new band uniform or what?"

"I have to stop by my house first," Sierra explained. "So, see you at California Dream?" she asked.

"See you there," Riley said with a grin. Her heart felt lighter all of a sudden.

When Riley walked into California Dream later that day, she saw Saul, the drummer, and Marta, the keyboardist, up on the stage. Marta was playing some chords and singing a cover of a Sheryl Crow song. Saul was drumming along.

Riley sat at a table and glanced around. No sign of Alex. Maybe he's backstage or something, she thought.

A waitress came by. "Can I get you anything?" she asked Riley.

"A cappuccino with skim milk, please," Riley said.

The Sheryl Crow song was over. Saul got up from his drum set, stepped up to the mike, and sang the next number. Riley was startled. It was "Don't You Know," the song Alex wrote for her. He sang it for the crowd at the party she and Riley threw at Larry's house a while back.

"*Pass her in the hall…Try to catch her smile…Don't you know you're all I need for a while? Make me want to change…Make me want to speak…Tell you how I feel…You're the one I seek….*"

As Riley listened to the song, she thought about Alex. Coming from Saul, the words didn't sound the same. In fact, it didn't feel as if the song was for her anymore.

Saul sang the chorus. "*Don't you know it's you, girl? Can't you hear the truth? Don't you know it's you? Can't I offer proof?*"

Where was Alex? Riley wondered. She couldn't help thinking about Willow's words in sewing class: *Alex told me.* When did they do all this talking, anyway?

The waitress brought Riley's cappuccino. Riley took a sip, barely tasting it. She glanced around, her mood plummeting by the second.

Riley looked at the phone booth in the corner of the room. Maybe she should check her answering machine. Maybe he called. Maybe—

Her thoughts were interrupted by the screech of

mike feedback and Saul's voice. "Let's take a short break and wait till Sierra gets here," he called out to Marta.

Saul trotted down the steps and headed for Riley's table. "Hey, Riley! What are you doing here?" He sounded breathless, and his face was shiny with sweat.

"I came here to, um, watch you guys rehearse," Riley said. "I ran into Sierra. She had to stop at her house, but she should be here soon." She smiled casually and added, "Where's Alex?"

Saul swiped a damp lock of hair from his forehead. "He called and said something important came up."

Riley frowned. "Something important? Like what?"

Saul shrugged. "Didn't say. Why?"

[**Riley: You don't think he'd be so low as to cancel our date and skip band practice to hang out with Willow, do you? I mean, Alex wouldn't do that...would he?**]

"Sorry I'm late, guys," Sierra said as she sauntered into California Dream. She was shaking her long red hair loose from her ponytail. Her guitar case was slung over one shoulder. "I got caught up practicing the violin piece I'm supposed to play for this citywide competition in a few weeks." She spotted Riley. "Hey, girl. You made it," she said, waving. Then she stopped and stared. "Rile? You look like you just saw a ghost. Are you okay?"

"Sure," Riley replied. "Actually, I'm not sure. Sit down, we need to talk. Two seconds—I promise."

Sierra pulled up a chair. "What's up?" she asked.

"What do you know about Willow Sweet?" Riley asked her. "Be honest."

Sierra frowned at Riley. She seemed to be considering something. "Willow used to hang out with Alex, like, last year," she said after a moment.

"Hang out?" Riley asked her. "Didn't they *go* out?"

Sierra sighed. "Okay. So I guess you know. They used to date."

"Alex told me," Riley said. "Why did they break up, though? He didn't tell me that."

[Riley: **Please say that Willow turned out to be a crazy lunatic, and they had a huge fight, and they split up. Please, please, please.**]

"Willow and Alex broke up because her dad got a temporary assignment in London, so her family had to move away," Sierra explained.

"Oh," Riley said.

"Alex was pretty devastated," Sierra went on. "After she moved, he—" She stopped. She seemed to realize that she'd said too much. "I mean, well…listen, you don't need to worry. He's totally over her now."

Yeah, right, Riley thought. She remembered how Alex dropped her hand yesterday, the moment he saw Willow running toward them.

He wasn't over her. He wasn't over her at all.

chapter
eight

Chloe trotted down the stairs, waving her fingers in the air so that her topcoat of Pink Glitter nail polish wouldn't smudge. She could hear Manuelo making dinner in the kitchen. It smelled like pasta with pesto, one of her favorites. The house smelled a lot better it did last night, when she was trying to execute Manuelo's beef stroganoff recipe.

That's exactly what I did with it. I executed it, Chloe thought glumly. Oh, well, that's ancient history. From now on—I swear on my stack of 'N Sync CDs—no more lies and deception.

At the bottom of the stairs, she could hear voices coming from the living room. Riley was talking to someone in hushed tones. It sounded like…Larry.

Larry?

"I figured out how to get Bob and Juan to lay off. The plan is…" The words faded away.

Chloe frowned. She was curious. What were her sister and Larry talking about?

Chloe inched around the banister and crept to the living room doorway. She peeked around the corner. Larry and Riley were sitting on the couch, their heads bent close.

"What have you got for me?" Riley was saying to Larry.

"Feast your eyes on this," Larry said triumphantly.

He had several rolled-up sheets of paper in his hand. He unrolled them on the coffee table.

Riley gasped. "Wow, these are awesome," she said.

"Hey, you're dealing with a pro," Larry said, winking.

Riley dropped her voice and said something else to Larry. Chloe tried to get even closer, but she couldn't hear what Riley was saying.

A few minutes later, Larry got up from the couch. "We're square, then?" He held out his right hand.

Riley shook it. "We're square."

"Good luck tomorrow night."

"Thanks, Larry. It's a pleasure doing business with you."

Larry walked to the back door. Chloe slipped into the shadows so he wouldn't see her. As soon as he was gone, she pounced on Riley in the living room.

"Okay, spill!" Chloe demanded. "What were you and Larry talking about? It sounded totally top secret."

Riley's eyes widened. "Oh, um, nothing important. Just some homework and stuff." She grabbed the sheets of paper lying on the coffee table and quickly rolled them up.

Chloe examined her sister. Riley's left eye started twitching. It always did that when she was lying.

"No way. I don't think so," Chloe said. "Come on, Riley. Spill it."

Riley sighed. She unrolled the papers. "Oh, all right."

"Cool!" Chloe rubbed her hands together and took a look.

They were sketches—really great sketches—of some really great evening dresses. "Did you draw these?" Chloe asked, surprised.

"Not exactly," Riley admitted. "These are the sketches Mom and Dad wanted me to do for the *Herald* interview tomorrow. They think I'm some sort of a future hotshot designer because of that apron they think I made...thanks to you," she added.

Chloe frowned. "You didn't do these sketches? So who did?" Then it came to her. "Aha! Larry."

"We kind of made this deal," Riley explained.

"But, Riley! That's totally dishonest!" Chloe cried.

[Chloe: Yeah, yeah, I know what you're thinking. I'm not exactly the Queen of Honesty. But I'm through with lying, remember?]

"Don't you feel bad about lying to Mom and Dad?" Chloe went on.

"M-m-me?" Riley sputtered. "What about you? I

heard you got an A plus in cooking today. Amanda told me. I'd like to hear how you managed that, when you don't even know how to boil water! Or is that *broil* water? I know you can't tell the difference."

Chloe felt heat rise in her cheeks. "I…uh…" She glanced toward the kitchen, where Manuelo was banging pots and pans around and singing the song, "Oklahoma!" She lowered her voice so he wouldn't overhear. "We had this assignment," she whispered. "We were supposed to make our favorite dish. I tried to make Manuelo's beef stroganoff, but, well, you know what happened. I was desperate. So I kind of borrowed one of Manuelo's Meals in a Minute."

"So then how can you accuse *me* of being dishonest?" Riley cried. "You're being dishonest, too!"

"That's different," Chloe shot back.

"How is that different?"

"It just is!"

"No way!" Riley cried. "You're totally cheating, too. You're supposed to cook your own—"

"What is going on in here?" Mrs. Carlson demanded, walking into the room. Pepper was close behind her, yipping loudly. "What are you two yelling about?"

"We're not yelling," Riley said immediately. "We were just talking about Chloe's cooking class."

"Oh?" Mom asked. "What about your class, Chloe?"

Chloe glanced at her mom. Then she glared at her sister.

"Chloe was just telling me that she got an A plus in cooking today," Riley announced.

Chloe frowned. Thanks a lot, Riley, she thought.

Mrs. Carlson beamed at Chloe. "Really? Honey, that's wonderful!"

"Thanks a lot, Mom," Chloe said as brightly as she could.

[Chloe: Yeah, so Mom thinks I'm a great cook. It wouldn't be so bad if she didn't have that gleam in her eye. Mom's planning something, and I have a feeling it involves me. Not good.]

"Chloe, I just had an idea," Mrs. Carlson said. "And it involves you."

[Chloe: See?]

"Why don't you make dinner tomorrow night for the Herald interview? I'm sure the reporter would love that," Mrs. Carlson finished.

Riley grabbed their mother's arm. "What a great idea! Chloe, isn't that a great idea?"

Chloe glared at Riley. How could she? "Yeah, great," she said.

"Fabulous!" Mrs. Carlson said. "I have to talk to Manuelo about place settings. And linens and silver and candles and flowers, too. Manuelo!" She disappeared down the hall.

Chloe was so angry, she wanted to yell at her sister.

But she didn't have time. She had to get busy figuring out how she was going to learn to cook—by tomorrow.

"I can't go through with this," Mr. Carlson said, covering his face with his hands.

It was Wednesday night. He, Mrs. Carlson, and Riley were sitting on the living room couch, waiting for Maria Rodriguez to show up.

Riley couldn't believe it. Her dad was usually so calm and relaxed. But tonight, he seemed more wound-up than Mom.

Manuelo was in the dining room, setting the table. Chloe was in the kitchen, cooking. Riley was dying to go in there and see what her sister was up to.

Mrs. Carlson glanced nervously at her watch, then at her husband. "What do you mean, you can't go through with this, Jake? The reporter will be here in five minutes."

"As soon as I started looking at my old sketches, all the pressure came flooding back," Mr. Carlson moaned. "The chest pains, the nausea, the irritable-bowel syndrome. Six months of meditation, right out the window."

"Dad, maybe you should take a deep breath or something," Riley suggested.

"Jake, I can't do this interview without you," Mrs. Carlson told him.

"Of course you can. You're great at interviews," Mr. Carlson pointed out.

"Yeah, but the H*erald* doesn't want just me. They want us as a couple. And I promised Maria Rodriguez you'd be here," Mrs. Carlson pleaded.

Mr. Carlson frowned. "We're not exactly a couple."

Mrs. Carlson waved her hand. "A minor technicality. We don't need to mention that little fact to Maria Rodriguez. Besides, she thinks you're fabulous!"

Mr. Carlson's face lit up. "Fabulous? Really? What else did she say?"

"Just that she thought your line of T-shirt fashions was groundbreaking," Mrs. Carlson told him.

"It *was* groundbreaking. Cotton tees for everyday wear, silk tees for evening. And for business, the T-suit," Mr. Carlson said proudly.

"You guys keep talking fashion," Riley said, jumping up from the couch. "I'm going to check on Chloe."

"Fine, dear," Mr. and Mrs. Carlson said at the same time.

Riley passed Manuelo in the dining room. He was carefully arranging white gardenias and floating candles in a shallow bowl of water. "It's perfect, no?" Manuelo said to Riley. "Or do you think I should add a few baby roses, too? Would Miss Macy like that?"

"It's perfect," Riley reassured him. "She'll love it."

Riley walked into the kitchen—and stopped in her tracks. Chloe was on the phone, talking in a low voice.

"I ordered the pad thai an hour ago!" Chloe whispered to the person on the other end. "It's supposed to be here by now. Can't you beep your delivery person or something?"

Riley glanced around. She saw that the trash can was overflowing with empty white paper containers. She couldn't believe it. Instead of cooking dinner for the family and Maria Rodriguez, Chloe was ordering massive amounts of takeout!

Chloe whirled around and saw Riley standing there. "Gotta call you back," Chloe said, hanging up. "Hey, sis! What's up?" she said in a too-bright voice. "That was Amanda. We were just... talking about that killer English quiz."

"This is the dinner you're supposed to cook for the reporter?" Riley asked, pointing at the garbage can. "Takeout?"

"Don't tell Mom and Dad," Chloe begged. "If you do, I'll...I'll tell them about Larry's sketches."

"You wouldn't dare!" Riley gasped, then sighed. Yes, she would. And Riley would deserve it. It was her fault that Chloe was in this mess. "Okay, it's a deal."

The phone rang. Chloe grabbed it. "Is this Holy Basil Thai Palace?" she whispered fiercely. "Where is my pad thai? What?"

She clamped a hand over her mouth. "Oh, hey, Travis, how are you? I'm sorry, I thought you were someone else."

Riley had to stifle a giggle. On the other hand, what was she laughing about? Her own love life was in the toilet.

The doorbell rang. Pepper began barking like mad.

"Chloe, how's that dinner coming?" Mrs. Carlson called from the other room. "Maria Rodriguez is here!"

"Riley, honey, your sketches!" Mr. Carlson added.

"…Oh, no, not much," Chloe was telling Travis. "Listen, I'd really love to talk, but I'm kind of in the middle of something. I'll call you later, okay? Bye!"

Chloe hung up, then threw Riley a look of pure misery. "Of course Travis would have to call me while I'm cooking dinner for Mom and Dad's superimportant interview," she complained.

"Yeah, it's so hard to cook when you're tied up on the phone and all those takeout places can't call you back," Riley teased.

Riley ducked as Chloe flung a dishrag in her direction.

"Okay, okay," Riley said, holding up her hands. "That reporter person is here. We need to come through for Mom and Dad. What do you say we call a truce and help each other survive the evening?"

Chloe sighed and smiled. "Okay, truce. And after tonight—no more lies."

Riley shook her head. "Definitely not."

Then the two sisters went into action mode. First, Riley helped Chloe empty the coconut-lemongrass soup into white bowls, put them on trays, and carry them into the dining room.

Maria Rodriguez was standing at the table. She was a tall, slender woman with shoulder-length black hair and a loosely tailored black suit. Mrs. Carlson had taken some of the sketches and spread them out on the table.

"And this is the budding designer," Mrs. Carlson said, beaming at Riley.

"These sketches are fabulous!" Maria gushed. "So original! Bud, get a shot of these."

A bald, middle-aged guy with a camera appeared from the living room. He sauntered to the table, focused, and took half a dozen shots of the sketches. "Got 'em," he mumbled.

Riley gulped as she realized that the sketches were going to be published. Her lie sat heavy in her stomach.

"And this is our chef, Chloe," Mr. Carlson spoke up, gesturing to Chloe.

"Hi, nice to meet you," Chloe said to Maria and Bud.

"Mmm, that looks fabulous," Maria said, glancing at the bowls of soup. "I love Thai food. Bud, get a shot of the table, will you?"

Bud clicked obediently.

The seven of them—Mr. and Mrs. Carlson, Manuelo, Bud, Maria Rodriguez, Chloe, and Riley—sat down to dinner. Bud kept clicking away. Maria took lots of small notes in a notebook.

"Chloe," Manuelo said after he'd taken a sip of soup. "Where did you…I mean, how did you…I mean, that cooking class must be really *fantastico*! Perhaps I should sign up?"

"We're so proud of her, aren't we, Jake?" Mrs. Carlson said, smiling radiantly at Chloe.

Riley glanced at Chloe. Her sister was blushing and squirming. Riley could tell that Chloe was as uncomfortable with the deception as she was.

Riley caught Chloe's eye and whispered, "Say 'Thank you.'"

"Thank you!" Chloe said automatically. Riley gave her a thumbs-up. They were going to get through this evening yet!

The second course was crispy duck with scallions. I could get used to Chloe's "cooking" every night, Riley thought, chowing down on the delicious food. The third course, the pad thai, finally showed up at the back door. Riley distracted Maria and the others with stories about her design inspirations while Chloe dealt with the delivery person.

"And, um, I get a lot of ideas from, you know, watching TV," Riley said. "And joggers. I get a lot of ideas from joggers. I'm thinking of designing an evening dress that's based on, um, a jogging bra with…you know, a skirt attached."

"Brilliant!" Maria said, scribbling.

Chloe returned with a huge platter of steaming noodles. "Pad thai!" she announced.

Everyone clapped. This evening is going really well, Riley thought, amazed.

"Do you find it difficult working together?" Maria asked Mr. and Mrs. Carlson as they were finishing the third course.

Mr. Carlson squirmed. "Well, uh, you know…"

"We make it work," Mrs. Carlson cut in with a tense-looking smile. "It's all about compromises and knowing your priorities. And, of course, scheduling."

"Sched-ul-ing," Maria said, scribbling in her notebook. "And what about your talented daughters? Do you ever think about including them in the family business, too? Certainly Riley, with her incredible talent. And what about Chloe? She could open a catering business."

Gulp! What was Mom going to say? Riley wondered.

"Oh, well, we haven't thought that far into the future," Chloe piped up. "Got to finish high school first. Education is so important!"

"Yes, so important!" Riley echoed. "As a matter of fact, I should be getting to my homework. You know me—study, study study!"

"What bright girls you have, Macy." Maria scribbled something else in her notebook.

"Me, too!" Chloe said. "Got a big test tomorrow. May I be excused?" she asked, standing.

Mrs. Carlson stared curiously at Riley and Chloe. "Well, all right…."

"Great. See you!" Riley left the table with her sister, grateful that the interview was over and that they'd never have to do this again.

chapter
nine

The next day Riley adjusted her backpack on her shoulders and strolled down the hall toward French class. She was wearing the new red T-shirt and black skirt she got at the mall last weekend. She was even wearing a new pair of platform boots.

That was going to be her theme for the day. Out with the old, in with the new.

She'd decided this morning that it was time for new things. That included a new attitude about the Alex-Willow situation. She was going to face it head on. She would just come right out and ask Alex about it. Sure, she'd be hurt if he wanted to get back together with Willow. On the other hand, maybe the whole thing was a misunderstanding.

Riley came to a screeching halt as she rounded a corner. Alex was standing by his locker, stuffing a bunch of books into his backpack and talking to Willow. The two of them were whispering and laughing about something.

Willow was wearing a tight black dress and high boots. Every few seconds, she touched Alex's arm.

Riley felt the familiar knot in her stomach tighten. She had to admit it. She was jealous of this girl. But who wouldn't be?

Riley took a deep breath, trying to gather her courage. Okay, she told herself, just walk up to them and ask him. Ask him what the deal is. If Alex doesn't want to be with me, I don't want to be with him.

[**Riley**: **So maybe that's not exactly how I feel at the moment, but it's how I want to feel. I get points for that, don't I?**]

"Riley! Hey!" Willow motioned her over.

Riley gritted her teeth and walked toward them. This kind of ruins the effect of storming up to them, she thought.

Alex gave her a big grin. Riley gave him a chilly smile in return. He frowned, looking confused.

"Hey, Riley," Willow said. "Alex was just filling me in on some of the teachers here."

Yeah, I bet.

"He wasn't sure about Ms. Spoke," Willow went on, hugging her books to her chest. "She seemed okay the other day, but do you like her? Do you think I'll like her class, or should I switch to something else while I can still escape? By the way, I love your outfit," she added. "You have the best taste in clothes."

"Thanks," Riley said, startled. How could Willow be so nice to her when she, Riley, had just caught Willow trying to steal Alex away? "Um, Ms. Spoke's fine. It's a fun class. You should probably stay, unless sewing isn't your thing."

"Thanks for the advice. That is so helpful," Willow said. She waved to Riley and Alex. "Well, I should be going. Bye!"

After Willow left, Riley looked at Alex. She couldn't bring herself to confront him. "I've gotta go, too," she mumbled, and she turned to leave.

Alex reached out and grabbed her arm. "Listen, Riley," he said in a low voice, "I am so sorry about canceling our date Tuesday night. And I'm sorry I couldn't apologize in person yesterday. I was out with this twenty-four-hour flu thing."

He was sick? Riley thought. "Are you okay now?" she asked him.

Alex nodded. "I'm fine. A hundred percent. Anyway, let me make it up to you. Do you want to get together tomorrow after school?"

He was looking at her so pleadingly that Riley's heart melted. "Um, sure. That would be great," she said, smiling shyly, then getting the courage to ask him about Willow. "Listen, I have to ask you something—"

"Hey, Alex! Riley!"

Riley glanced up. Willow had doubled back. Bad timing!

"I totally forgot to ask you," Willow called out. "Do you two want to come over to my house tomorrow after school and swim in our pool?"

Alex shook his head. "Thanks, Willow, but I've got other plans."

Riley smiled at Alex, knowing that his "other plans" were with her. And maybe, just maybe, she should be gracious about it.

"Sorry," Riley told Willow. "I have plans, too. Let's do it another time."

Chloe and Amanda were busy making today's cooking assignment: apple pie. The classroom was filled with the yummy smells of fruit, cinnamon, and nutmeg. Mr. Ferguson was up front, helping a couple of students with their crusts.

Chloe yawned. She had gotten up today at 5:00 A.M. in order to take out the trash before Manuelo got up. She couldn't let him see the dozens of containers from last night, or he would have figured out her fabulous meal was a fake.

In any case, it was worth it. The dinner had been a huge success. And afterward, she and Riley had sealed their truce with a pinkie-promise—no more lies and deception!

"Chloe, what are you doing?" Amanda called out.

Chloe glanced up from her work. She realized that she had bits of raw piecrust stuck to her rolling pin, her cutting board, her clothes, her face, and her hair. As hard as she tried, she couldn't get a nice, smooth piecrust going. Unlike Amanda, who had turned out a perfect crust and was now carving her initials into the top of her pie.

"Oh, I'm just, um, making my pie," Chloe said, smiling feebly.

"Do you want some help?" Amanda asked her.

"I'm fine. Really! This piecrust thing just takes some practice," Chloe said cheerfully.

But deep down, Chloe knew that her pie was hopeless. Even if she was lucky and managed to finish it before class ended, it was destined to look like a hideous mutant pie from outer space.

But it would be *her* hideous mutant pie from outer space. It would be worth getting a C (or D or even an F) if it meant getting the grade on her own.

Mr. Ferguson strolled by. He stared quizzically at Chloe's pie. "Ms. Carlson, you seem not to be at the top of your game today," he said.

"Bad hair day," Chloe explained. "It affects everything I do."

Mr. Ferguson frowned and kept walking.

Chloe finished putting together her pie as best she could and slid it into one of the ovens. At the end of class, she went over to check on it.

[Chloe: So, I'm kind of afraid to look at the thing, but the door swings open all on its own! The rack slides out of the oven. And there it is. I was right. It is a hideous alien creature! All wrinkled and brown and oozing. It winks one of its three eyes at me and says, "Greetings, earthling. I am from the Galaxy Red Delicious, and I have come to rule over your planet...."]

Mr. Ferguson didn't make any comments about Chloe's pie looking like an alien. But he did give her a C. "Perhaps your hair will be in a better mood tomorrow," he said. "Let's hope so, anyway."

"Thanks, Mr. Ferguson!" Chloe told him.

The bell rang. Chloe started frantically cleaning up.

"Hey, Chloe!"

Chloe turned around. Travis was standing there.

"Oh, hey." Chloe quickly threw a dishrag over her pie. She didn't want him to think that she was a less-than-talented cook. After all, she'd won him over with her brownies—okay, Amanda's brownies—the other day.

"Mmm. Your pie smells delicious," he said, pointing at Amanda's creation, which was sitting next to Chloe's.

Chloe glanced at the pie, then at Amanda, who was chatting with Mr. Ferguson across the room. She knew that Travis probably wanted a piece. "Oh, um, thanks," she replied, cringing as she said it. "I'd offer you some, but it's still too hot. So anyway, how are you?" she asked, pulling a little clump of raw piecrust out of her hair.

"Not bad," Travis replied. "I was wondering…you want to go to the beach with me on Sunday?"

Chloe stopped tugging at her hair and stared at him. "Yes!" she said happily. "Wow, the beach! I'll bring a picnic!"

She clamped a hand over her mouth. What was she saying? She didn't know how to cook. How was she going to put a picnic together?

Just slap together some peanut butter and jelly sandwiches. How hard can that be? she reassured herself.

"Great!" Travis said, nodding. "I was beginning to think you didn't want to go out or something. Anyway, that's cool about the picnic. You're such an awesome cook. In case you're interested, my favorite foods are grilled cheese sandwiches and double-chunk chocolate chip cookies. Can you handle that?" he asked with a smile.

"Oh, no problem," Chloe told him.

"Really?" Travis said. "Cool. I'll make something, too. See you later!"

As soon as he was gone, Chloe raced across the room to her friend. "Amanda, do you know how to make grilled cheese?" she asked.

chapter
ten

On Friday morning, Manuelo spread the front page of the *Malibu Herald*'s lifestyle section across the kitchen table. "I am so proud of you girls," he said. "Color photographs. Look at Chloe holding a platter of her famous pad thai!"

Mrs. Carlson leaned over his shoulder. "And look at Riley's magnificent sketches. I have to call Jake right away. He's probably busy doing his alternate-nostril yoga breathing exercises." She headed to the phone.

Chloe spooned a bite of Manuelo's cranberry-mango oatmeal into her mouth and scanned the article. She had to admit, she did look good in the picture. She wondered if Travis's family got the *Herald*. She wondered if Travis would see her picture.

[Chloe: ACT TWO, SCENE ONE: Travis Morgan cuts Chloe Carlson's picture out of the *Malibu Herald*, ever-so-carefully, with a pair of scissors.

He tapes it to his locker door. He stares at it longingly, one hand over his heart. He's in love!]

"Wow, I look really good," Riley murmured. "I'm so glad I wore my new top that day."

"Mom and Dad look pretty good, too," Chloe pointed out. There was a big photo of Jake and Macy Carlson sitting on the couch, holding up several outfits they had designed together. The caption under the photo read: DESIGN TEAM FINDS THEIR MARRIAGE A SOURCE OF INSPIRATION AND CREATIVITY!

Chloe leaned across the table. "Uh, Riley?" she whispered. "Why did Mom and Dad tell Maria Rodriguez that they're still together?"

"I don't know," Riley said. "For the same reason we told everybody that we knew how to cook and sew?"

Chloe shrugged. "Well, those days are totally over," she declared firmly. She thought about the beach picnic on Sunday. I'm going to cook that food all on my own, she swore to herself.

Riley leaned against her locker later that day and glanced at her watch for what seemed like the hundredth time. Alex was supposed to meet her fifteen minutes ago for their date. Where *was* he?

She crossed her arms over her chest as she thought about Alex. Guys were so weird. Sometimes they seemed as though they were really into you, and other times they acted as if they couldn't care less.

With Alex it was even more confusing. He had canceled their date on Tuesday with little explanation. And now, he seemed to be a no-show again. Plus, there was the Willow factor, which she still had to talk to him about.

Riley spotted Bob and Juan and another guy from the football team walking by. Tad or something. She realized that this was her golden opportunity to keep her promise to Larry.

"Hey, Riley," Bob said. "Do me a favor and apologize to Larry for us, okay?"

"Really?" Riley asked. Maybe this would be easier than she thought.

"Yeah," Juan said. "If Larry wants to be a girl, it's okay with us." He started snickering.

Bob and Tad soon followed. "Anything that'll get him out of our gym class is okay with us," Bob added, laughing.

Riley fumed. "For your information, it takes a lot of confidence for a guy to be in a sewing class. And, well, girls really like confidence in a guy," she said. "Did you know that the girls in sewing are practically lining up to date Larry?"

"You're kidding," Tad said.

Riley smiled. "Why do you think he joined the class in the first place?"

Bob looked stunned. "Wow," he said after a moment. "I totally underestimated that guy."

"Totally," Juan agreed.

As the three of them walked away, Riley heard Tad say, "I wonder if I can still switch out of metal shop and get into that sewing class."

Riley smiled to herself. Larry is *so* going to be their idol from now on. She glanced up and saw Alex trotting down the hall.

"Sorry I'm late!" he said breathlessly as he stopped by her side. "I was talking to a friend and totally lost track of the time. I really apologize!"

Was the friend Willow? Riley wanted to ask. But she didn't want to sound like a jealous freak. Instead, she simply smiled and said, "Don't worry about it. Let's go."

She and Alex headed to a pizza place first. After a couple of slices, they rented Rollerblades.

"You're great on those!" Alex called out as Riley sped down the boardwalk.

"Hey, I learned to do this before I learned to walk," Riley teased him.

They were having such a fun and relaxed time that Riley almost forgot about Willow. Almost. Was Willow the "friend" who made him late? Thinking about the possibility cast a shadow over their date.

It was almost dark by the time Alex walked Riley home. The sun was going down over the ocean, turning the water brilliant shades of orange and purple. A few faint stars twinkled in the twilight sky.

"You know one of the things I really like about you, Riley?" Alex said as they got to her doorstep. "You're so honest. I feel as though you always mean what you say."

Riley started. "Huh?"

Alex stopped and shook his head. "I can't stand liars," he said, a fierce edge in his voice. "Take Marta. She lied the other day about why she missed band practice, and we all found out. I mean, was that necessary? Why couldn't she just tell us the truth? That kind of behavior shows a total lack of respect for the rest of us, you know?"

"Yeah, sure," Riley muttered. But inside, she was wondering, did this mean Alex didn't lie about why he missed band practice on Tuesday? Maybe he had an honest excuse—an excuse having nothing to do with Willow.

She felt relief wash over her—until she reminded herself that she'd lied about her sewing project. Not only to her teacher, but to her parents and the reporter from the Herald.

Well, he'll never find out about that anyway. And she hoped nobody else would either.

Riley didn't have any time to dwell on that. She felt Alex putting his hands on her shoulders. She glanced up at him.

He was smiling a warm, dreamy smile at her. "I had a great time," he whispered.

Riley's heart began racing. Her shoulders felt all tingly where Alex was touching her. "Um, me, too," she whispered back.

And then, before she knew it, his head leaned

toward hers. Their lips touched. Every cell in her body felt as if it were on fire.

"Oops! Sorry! Do I have bad timing, or what?"

Riley yanked away from Alex, blushing. Chloe was coming up the walk, her backpack slapping against her shoulder.

Riley glared at her. "Hey, Chloe."

"Hey, Chloe!" Alex called out, stepping away from Riley. "I was just leaving."

He gave Riley a peck on the cheek and started down the street. "You coming to California Dream tomorrow night?" he asked, turning back.

"I'll be there," Riley said.

"Promise?"

"Promise."

Alex smiled and waved. Riley watched him disappear around the corner.

Chloe wiggled her eyebrows at Riley. "Well, well," she said. "Looks like someone's in loooove!"

"Oh, give me a break," Riley snapped. But inside, she didn't care if Chloe teased her. Alex's kiss was…perfect. And better yet, it told her exactly how Alex felt about her.

He*r*, not Willow. She realized she had nothing to worry about in the competition department.

"Come on, tell me everything," Chloe insisted. "Where did you go? What did you talk about? Is he a good kisser?"

"Stop it," Riley cried, blushing again. The girls walked in the front door.

Mrs. Carlson was standing there. "Guess what?" she practically screamed.

Riley and Chloe exchanged a glance.

"Mom, take a deep breath," Chloe said quickly. "Are you okay? Maybe we should get some of those meditation tapes from Dad."

"No, no, you don't understand!" Mrs. Carlson screeched. "We're going to be on TV!"

"What?" Riley gasped.

Mrs. Carlson went on to explain that she just got a call from Kendall Clark, who had seen the article in the *Herald*. "Kendall Clark—you know, as in, *At Home with Kendall Clark*," she said. "She wants to come here on Sunday afternoon and interview the entire family! Isn't that fabulous?" She grabbed both girls and began twirling them around. "You can cook again, Chloe, the way you did for Maria Rodriguez. And you, Riley, can do some sketches right there in front of the cameras! We're all going to be famous!"

Sketch…on TV? Riley stared at Chloe in horror.

Chloe had an equal look of terror on her face. "Cook…on TV?" she squeaked.

All the warm, fuzzy feelings Riley had from Alex's kiss were gone. They were quickly replaced by a new emotion: dread.

chapter
eleven

Chloe paced back and forth across the kitchen floor the next morning, trying to work up her courage. She was eating a blueberry muffin for breakfast and rehearsing her speech at the same time. Pepper sat on the floor, watching her progress intently. Chloe wasn't sure if the dog was listening to her speech or hoping for crumbs.

"Listen, Travis," she said out loud. "I know I said we'd go on a picnic tomorrow afternoon. But something's come up." She shook her head. "No, that's not right."

She took another bite of her blueberry muffin, then resumed her speech.

"Hey, Travis," she said, smiling at Pepper. Maybe this would go better if she used the dog as a stand-in. "How's it going? Beautiful day, isn't it? Listen, I heard the weather forecast, and the weather guy said there might, um, be a tornado or whatever tomorrow. So what do you say we have our picnic today instead?"

The phone rang. Oh, no, it's him, Chloe thought. She picked it up on the fourth ring. "Hello?"

"Hey, it's me. Amanda."

Chloe let her breath out in a big whoosh. "Amanda! What's up? Tell me how I should break it to Travis that I can't go out with him tomorrow."

"Travis asked you out?" Amanda cried. "Cool! Why didn't you tell me?"

"I can't believe I didn't tell you!" Chloe replied. "Amanda, everything is so messed up. Twice now he's called me and I've had to hang up on him. He asked me out for pizza the other day, and I couldn't go because the kitchen was on fire. And—"

"On *fire*?" Amanda repeated.

"Never mind. Long story. Anyway, bottom line, I'm worried that Travis is getting the wrong impression. I mean, I really do want to go out with him. You know that more than anybody."

Amanda sighed. "Look. Just be straight with him. Tell him why you have to cancel. Make sure you suggest a time you can reschedule for. Okay?"

"Okay," Chloe said. "Thanks, Amanda. I should always listen to you."

Amanda giggled. "Definitely."

After hanging up, Chloe took another deep breath and dialed Travis's number. One ring, two rings...

"Hello?"

"Hey, Travis? It's Chloe."

"Oh, hey, how's it going?" Travis said happily. "I was just polishing my bike. You should see it. I got this new kind of wax, and the red paint really shines like—"

"Listen, Travis," Chloe blurted out nervously. "I have to cancel our date tomorrow. You see, I'm going to be on TV and—"

"Give me a break," Travis replied. "First there's a fire in your kitchen, and now you're going to be on TV? Why don't you just tell me the truth, Chloe? You don't want to go out with me."

"But I do!" Chloe cried out.

"Right. Well, I have to go. I'm visiting my grandmother today," he said abruptly.

Chloe was beginning to panic. Stay cool, she told herself. "Okay, well, then, maybe another time?" she said in a friendly voice.

"Whatever." Travis hung up without saying good-bye.

Chloe replaced the receiver slowly. That was *not* what I had in mind, she thought.

That night, Riley was almost late for Alex's gig at California Dream. She spent more time than she realized combing her closet for the perfect outfit. She finally settled on black Lycra pants, a black top, and black boots.

[Chloe: I helped her pick it out. Mom always says, "When in doubt, wear black." So do I.]

After a last check in the mirror, Riley went tearing out of the house.

As she approached the beach club, she could hear the sound of a bass guitar blasting away. Another guitar joined in, then drums, and then she could hear Sierra singing.

The club was packed. The seats inside and on the outdoor deck over the beach were all taken, and there were hardly any empty spots on the sand, either. Riley saw Carrie, Joelle, Tara, and some other girls from school hanging out on a blanket, and she waved hi. They waved back.

Riley threaded her way through the crowd and tried to find a spot inside where she could stand and watch Alex. Sierra was strutting across the stage, singing a song about broken hearts.

"You told me that you loved me. You told me that you were mine. But now we're apart. You broke my heart…So now it's payback time…"

Sierra looked awesome in a sequin-and-rhinestone tube top and a tight black leather skirt. The sequins and rhinestones flashed and glittered in the spotlight every time she moved.

Sierra onstage never ceased to amaze Riley. She completely let go when she performed. She spun around, danced, kicked her heels up in the air. She sang with her heart and soul. Riley loved watching her.

Alex was onstage, too, dressed in a black T-shirt and

black jeans, his head bent low over his guitar. He looked so hot. There was no other word for it. Riley remembered his kiss from last night, and her heart began beating faster.

She found a column to lean against and settled there. She had a perfect view of Sierra—and of Alex.

Sierra was a ball of fire, whirling, kicking, spinning. *"You told me that you loved me…You told me that you were mine…."*

The crowd was going wild for her, clapping and singing along. The energy in the place was intense.

Riley glanced around the room, spotting kids she knew here and there.

And then, all of a sudden, her eyes zoned in on a familiar figure. Perfect figure, perfect superblond hair, perfect white sundress…

Willow was standing across the club, sipping a bottle of mineral water and bobbing her head to the beat. She was with a girl Riley didn't know. The girl leaned over to Willow and pointed at Alex. The two of them began giggling.

For a second, Riley thought about going over and joining Willow and the other girl. But something held her back. She wasn't quite ready to be buddies with Willow yet. Maybe in a week or two, after things had progressed further with Alex and she was feeling more secure with him.

Fifteen minutes later, Chloe and Amanda showed

up at California Dream. "What did we miss?" Chloe asked Riley.

"A great song. Hey, see that girl?" Riley whispered, pointing to Willow. "What do you think of her?"

"Gwyneth Paltrow," Amanda said immediately.

"No, I'd say she's more like Cameron Diaz," Chloe said, nodding. "Who is she? Can I hate her? I hate her."

This was not what Riley had in mind. "Her name's Willow," Riley explained. "She used to go out with Alex."

"Oh." Chloe said. "Well, she's got nothing on you. Don't worry about her. Besides, after that kiss I witnessed yesterday—"

"Kiss?" Amanda giggled. "Tell me more!"

"It's obvious Alex is really into you," Chloe finished.

Riley felt herself blushing.

The three girls fell silent as Sierra broke into a really soulful song. Riley eventually forgot about Willow and lost herself in the music—and in watching Alex.

The Wave played for over an hour. During the final number—a seriously loud song—the crowd got to their feet, clapping and screaming.

"Amanda and I are going to go grab some sodas," Chloe yelled over the music. "Do you want to come with us, Riley?"

Riley shook her head. "I want to say hi to Alex."

Chloe gave her a thumbs-up. "Have fun!"

Riley waved good-bye to Chloe and Amanda, then tried to inch around people so she could get backstage.

"Hey, watch it," a burly guy snapped as she tried to pass him. A girl bumped into her, spilling her soda all over Riley's boots.

Frustrated, Riley tried to make her way past the mob so she could get to the band. It took forever. Finally, she reached the stage and trotted up the stairs.

People were milling around Sierra and the other band members. Riley craned her neck, trying to find Alex.

He was there, near the back of the stage. Riley smiled and waved. And then her smile froze on her face.

Alex and Willow seemed to be having some kind of intense-looking conversation.

Confused, Riley stepped back into the shadows to watch.

Alex reached up and removed the gold earring he always wore.

Riley held her breath. What's going on?

Alex handed the earring to Willow. She took it from him and put it on.

Then she threw her arms around Alex, and the two of them hugged.

chapter
twelve

Riley watched in horror as Alex held his old girl-friend in his arms.

[Riley: What was that song Sierra was singing about broken hearts? That's me. I'm there. I'm there right now, right at this second, thanks to that two-timing Alex and that back-stabbing Willow.]

Before she had a chance to change her mind, Riley stormed to the back of the stage. "Hey, Rile!" she heard Sierra call out. But she didn't stop to talk to her friend.

Alex and Willow were just finishing their marathon hug when Riley marched up to them.

"Why?" she said, glaring at Alex. "Why didn't you just tell me the truth?"

Alex stared at her blankly. "Truth? What are you talking about, Riley?"

"Hey, Riley," Willow said, pushing back a lock of her

perfect platinum-blond hair. "Is something wrong?"

Riley glanced at Willow's right earlobe. She had seen correctly. Willow was now wearing Alex's earring.

"Please don't lie to me anymore, Alex," Riley cried out. "Didn't you tell me that you hate liars?"

"Lie? About what?" Alex looked totally confused.

Riley pointed to the earring. "You gave Willow your earring. What? Are you going steady or something now? After you told me it was over between the two of you?"

Riley was vaguely aware that Sierra, Saul, and Marta had fallen silent and were listening. Well, she didn't care.

Alex put his hands on Riley's shoulders. "No, no, listen," he said gently. "You don't understand. Willow gave me that earring last year as a present. After we broke up, she told me to keep it—you know, as a friendship thing. But now that things are, well, different..." He paused and gazed deeply into Riley's eyes. "I felt weird wearing it. Even as a friendship thing. So I gave it back to her."

"It was kind of an emotional good-bye moment," Willow piped up. "That's why I hugged him. That's all it was, Riley—honest!"

Riley stared at Alex. He was clearly telling the truth. She felt blood rushing into her face.

[Riley: **Is this the most embarrassing moment of my life? Hmm. There was that time when I was two and my diaper fell off at the mall. And there was the time a few years ago when I walked** around school all day with a huge strawberry jam stain on the front of my shirt. Other than that, yes, I think this might qualify as THE most embarrassing moment of my life.]

Willow put a hand on Riley's arm. "Look, I'm really glad to have the earring back. I'm also glad to have Alex as a friend—and you, too, Riley." She gave Riley a hug.

"Listen, I am so sorry to go off like that," Riley mumbled into Willow's hair.

"No problem," Willow said. She stepped back and smiled at Riley. "Anyway, I think this is my cue to go. See you guys later!"

Willow took off. Thankfully, Sierra was doing some damage control on the stage and distracting everyone with a story about her first gig at California Dream.

"And then both my shoes went flying into the air. Except they weren't my shoes. They were these expensive designer shoes that I'd borrowed from my friend's mom...."

Riley turned to Alex. "I am so sorry," she whispered. "I feel like an idiot."

"Don't worry about it," Alex said, smiling. He lowered his voice. "I mean, I have zero interest in Willow—or any other girl—except you. Ever since I met you, well, you know..."

Riley blushed as he wrapped her in his arms and gave her a long hug. Then he kissed her on the lips— softly, gently.

Riley's head was spinning with happiness. She knew once and for all that Alex wanted her, not Willow.

"Ahem."

Riley and Alex broke apart. Sierra was standing there.

"Sorry to interrupt, but, Alex, we need to go over next week's rehearsal schedule before Marta leaves," Sierra told him. She smiled apologetically at Riley.

"No problem," Alex said. "I'll be right back. You'll be here, right?" he asked Riley.

"Sure," Riley said, blushing again and looking at the floor. She noticed a black backpack sitting in the corner. "Alex, is this yours?" she asked him.

Alex shook his head. "Nope. Must be someone else's. Anyone missing a backpack?" he called out. No one claimed it.

"Why don't you check inside it and see if there's any ID?" Alex suggested to Riley.

"Okay," she said, nodding.

Alex went into a huddle with Sierra and the other band members. Riley picked up the backpack and opened it. Inside, she saw a couple of textbooks and a spiral-bound notebook.

Riley pulled out the notebook. It had Willow's name on the cover. Willow must have forgotten her backpack, she said to herself, opening the book to the first page.

Riley gasped. Alex's name was written all over the page—with big pink hearts around it. *Alex + Willow 4-ever* was boldly written inside the largest heart of them all.

It all made sense now. Alex didn't want to get back together with Willow—but Willow most definitely wanted to get back with Alex.

"Hey, Riley!"

Riley shoved the notebook inside the backpack and glanced up. Willow was crossing the stage toward her.

"I just realized I forgot my backpack," Willow said. "Oh, there it is. You have it. Great! I was afraid someone might have stolen it or something."

Riley handed her the backpack. "No, no one stole it," she said slowly. The only one who's trying to do any stealing around here is you, she thought.

Willow beamed at her. "Thanks so much! See you Monday in class!"

"Yeah, see you," Riley said. She watched Willow walk away.

chapter
thirteen

"Set up Camera Two over there, Kevin. No, I said over there! Are the girls miked yet? And where is my iced tea with soy milk? I asked for it yesterday!"

Kendall Clark bustled around the living room of the Carlsons' house, barking orders. She was tiny and slim, with a long mane of curly black hair. She wore a baggy blue suit and carried a clipboard. Chloe wasn't sure why, but she found the woman terrifying.

Chloe glanced around nervously. The entire house had been taken over by cameras, cameramen, and various other people whose jobs she didn't quite understand. People were yelling things like "Sound check!" and "Lock up!" and flinging wires and cords around.

Kendall grabbed a mike from a guy who was running by. "At Home with Kendall Clark, testing one, two, three," she said. She looked up at Chloe. "You. You're one of the kids, right? Carly?"

"My name is Chloe," Chloe corrected her.

"You're going to be giving us a little cooking demonstration, right? Please keep it short, okay?" Kendall snapped. "Testing one, two…"

Riley came up to Chloe and grabbed her elbow. "What are we going to do?" she whispered. "We're, like, totally doomed!"

"Just between us, I'm going have to lie this one last time," Chloe whispered back. "I'm going to defrost one of Manuelo's Meals in a Minute and pretend it's mine."

Riley nodded. "I'm just going to redraw the sketches Larry did for the *Herald* interview. I've been practicing."

"Five minutes! Everybody, take your places!" a man in an *At Home with Kendall Clark* T-shirt called out.

Mrs. Carlson came running downstairs in a gray suit. "How do I look? Do I look okay? I can't believe we're going to be on TV. I'm so nervous!"

"You look great, Mom," Chloe reassured her. "Take a breath. Take a bunch of breaths."

Mrs. Carlson sucked in a breath and nodded. "Good, that worked for me. Where's your father?"

"Right here." Jake Carlson sauntered in from the kitchen. He was holding a large, gaudy-looking trophy.

"What's that?" Riley asked him, curious.

"This was my first design award," Mr. Carlson said proudly. "I thought it might be good for the interview."

"Places, everyone!" someone yelled.

Chloe, Riley, Mr. Carlson, and Mrs. Carlson plopped

down on the living room couch. Kendall Clark assumed her position on one of the side chairs.

Kendall smiled at Mr. Carlson. "I am such a huge fan of yours," she gushed. "You are a genius!"

Mr. Carlson blushed and grinned. "Oh, well, I'm not—do you really think so? Listen, would you like to see my trophy?" He pulled it out from behind his back and plunked it down on the coffee table.

"Half that trophy is mine, you know," Mrs. Carlson reminded him. She smiled tightly at Kendall. "We do everything as a team."

Kendall turned to Riley. "Rita, right? You're going to be doing macramé crafts?"

"Riley," Riley corrected her. "I'm doing some sketches—"

"Honey, your mom and I thought that instead of the sketches, you should show everybody that apron you made in school," Mr. Carlson cut in. "It's so brilliant!"

"B-but—" Riley sputtered.

"Apron. Sounds great. Quick, easy visual." Kendall turned in her seat. "Kevin, where's my tea?" she yelled.

Chloe saw her sister's face turn white. She leaned over. "What's wrong, Riley?"

"I gave that apron back to Larry!" Riley whispered. She got up from the couch. "Excuse me, everybody, I have to make a quick phone call."

"But we're taping in a few minutes!" Mrs. Carlson cried out.

"Trust me, Mom, it's important," Riley told her.

Chloe followed Riley into the kitchen. Riley picked up the phone and punched in Larry's number. "Be home, be home, be home," Riley mumbled.

"What are you going to do if he's not?" Chloe whispered, glancing over her shoulder.

"Don't say that!" Riley's shoulders slumped. "Oh, no, I got his machine."

Chloe listened as Riley left Larry a long, urgent-sounding message. "Do you hear me, Larry?" Riley finished. "You have to bring the apron over. It's a major emergency. Got it?" She hung up and shook her head.

"Not to keep pointing out the obvious," Chloe said gently, "but what if he doesn't get your message in time?"

Riley sighed. "Then I'm cooked. I'm toast. I'm… I'm…I'm going to have to tell Mom and Dad the truth."

"Welcome to *At Home with Kendall Clark*. Today, we're coming to you from the home of Jake and Macy Carlson, fashion designers extraordinaire. You've seen their creations on MTV and on the runways. Now you can see how they work—and play—at their lovely beach home in Malibu!"

While Kendall talked, Riley kept peering out the window, trying to get a glimpse of Larry's house next door. It was totally dark. Where was he? He had to get home, get her message, and get over here as soon as possible!

Riley had a hard time paying attention to the interview. Kendall kept firing questions, and her parents kept interrupting and correcting each other.

"Actually, no, Jake, our first fashion show was in 1998."

"No, I think it was '97, Macy."

Chloe was in the kitchen, defrosting one of Manuelo's baggies of stroganoff. Manuelo was in the living room, hovering in the background, nodding proudly every time Mr. Carlson or Mrs. Carlson said anything.

"Trust me, Jake, I remember because of that incident with that model named Slush or whatever."

"Her name was Rain."

Riley glanced at her watch and tapped her foot. Come on, Larry, where *are* you?

All of a sudden, without warning, Kendall Clark turned to her. "Rhonda, your parents tell us that you're quite the budding designer yourself. Do you have one of your creations you can share with us?" she said brightly.

"Um…yes. I do. My chef's apron. But first, I think we should all go into the kitchen and taste my sister's wonderful cooking!" she improvised.

"Honey, that is so sweet that you want your sister to go first," Mr. Carlson praised her.

Kendall Clark nodded. "Let's go, then!"

She got up and walked to the kitchen. A dozen crew members followed with cameras, mikes, and bright lights.

"I'll be right with you all," Riley called out, waving. Then she made a beeline for the phone in the hallway, almost tripping over a big bunch of wires on the floor.

She picked up the phone and dialed Larry's number. "Come on, come on, come on!" she whispered.

"Hi, you've reached the Slotnicks. We can't take your call right now. But if you'll leave a message, one of us will call you right back." *Beeeeeep!*

"Larry!" Riley whispered into the phone. "Where are you? Please, please come over with that apron as soon as you can. Please!"

She hung up, sighed, and hurried to the kitchen.

Beeeeeep! Chloe rushed to the microwave and took out Manuelo's Baggie of beef stroganoff. Good, it was defrosted—finally! She frantically dumped the contents into a pan on the stove and began stirring.

[**Chloe:** I know, I know. I'm lying **AGAIN.** But this is the last time. I promise!]

The door banged open, and Kendall Clark waltzed in, followed by Mr. and Mrs. Carlson and Manuelo. A bunch of guys with cameras and mikes trailed after them.

Chloe felt like a deer caught in headlights. She wasn't ready for them yet! Then she remembered Manuelo's empty Baggie sitting on the counter. She quickly threw a dish towel over it and plastered on a smile for the camera.

"Uh, hi, everyone!" she said. "What's up?"

"And here we have Casey Carlson, Rhonda's twin sister, who we hear has a real flair for cooking," Kendall said, gesturing to Chloe. "What are we making, Casey?"

"Um, we're making beef stroganoff," Chloe said in a nervous voice. "Old family recipe."

"It's mine!" Manuelo piped up in the background.

More than you know, Chloe thought. Out loud, she said, "Um, if you'll all go into the dining room, I think we're ready to eat," she said.

The mob trailed into the dining room. Chloe began nervously ladling the stroganoff into bowls. If I can just get through this night, I swear on my entire pierced earring collection—no more lies! she promised herself.

"Hi, you've reached the Slotnicks. We can't take your call right now. But if you'll leave a message, one of us will call you right back!" *Beeeeeep*!

Riley slammed down the phone. She had left six messages for Larry. Obviously he wasn't home yet.

"Riley! Time for dinner, hon! And bring your apron, please!"

Her mother was calling her from the dining room. Time had run out. Riley would have to show up empty-handed and confess her terrible lie.

Okay, time to face the music, she thought gloomily.

When she walked into the dining room, she saw everyone sitting at the table: her parents at either end, Chloe and Manuelo next to each other, and Kendall Clark across from them. The camera crew was all over the place with their lights, cameras, and microphones.

"Where's your apron, sweetie?" Mr. Carlson asked.

"Mom, Dad, can I talk to you for a minute?" Riley said.

Riley's parents exchanged a glance. "Sure, honey," her mom said. "Excuse us for a moment, Kendall."

"Cut!" Kendall cried, obviously annoyed.

Mr. and Mrs. Carlson joined Riley in the kitchen.

"What is it, baby?" Mrs. Carlson asked her, looking concerned.

Riley sat at the kitchen table. "I didn't make that apron," she began.

Mr. Carlson frowned. "What are you saying?"

"I'm a sewing fraud," Riley went on. "Someone else made that apron. I happened have it on in sewing class, and the teacher thought it was mine. So she gave me an A-plus on the spot. And I...well, I didn't say anything."

Mrs. Carlson gasped. "Riley!"

"And these designs aren't mine, either," Riley said, pointing to Larry's sketches, which were laid out on the table. "I kind of borrowed them from a friend."

This is the lowest moment of my life, Riley thought. I should have told them straight out from the beginning. Instead, I let everything spiral out of control.

"What are we going to tell Kendall?" Riley asked.

"We'll just tell her that there's been a misunderstanding," Mr. Carlson said.

And when they returned to the dining room that's just what Riley's father did.

"What?" Kendall cried, rising from her seat. "Your kid isn't showing her sketches? This won't do. How am I supposed to re-focus my whole interview? This was supposed to be a family-oriented piece."

"I'm sure you can come up with something," Mrs. Carlson assured her. "You wouldn't have made it this far if you weren't *brilliant*."

Way to go, Mom, Riley thought. She could see that the talk show host was beginning to soften.

"And such a snazzy dresser," Mr. Carlson added. "So much, that we'd *love* to design something for you."

[Riley: Okay. I have to admit that my parents are pretty cool. After all, they're willing to stroke an overbearing talk-show host's ego just to save me from publicly humiliating myself. Now that's what I call unconditional love. And, hey, I think it's working.]

"Oh." Kendall smiled. "Well, I guess you're right." She sat back down. "You know, this whole family thing is so overplayed these days anyway. Maybe we should get back to basics. Just focus on the two superpower designers."

"Fabulous idea, Kendall," a cameraman said.

"Works for us," Mrs. Carlson agreed.

"Then it's settled," Kendall replied. "Let's take a break, eat, then start over." She turned to a cameraman. "Kevin, get some footage of me dining with Jake and

Macy," she said. "No need to get the kids in the shot."

Riley let out the breath she didn't know she was holding and sat down at the table.

"Do me a favor, though, Rhonda," Kendall added. "No more surprises, okay?"

"You got it," Riley said.

"Let's eat, already," Manuelo said.

Riley felt as though a huge weight had been lifted off her chest. The apron crisis seemed to have blown over. She and Chloe stared at each other and breathed sighs of relief.

As Kendall, Mr. Carlson, and Mrs. Carlson continued to talk about the suit they were going to design for the host, Kendall lifted a spoonful of stroganoff to her lips. Immediately, she spit it out. "Bleh! Ugh! What is that?" she shouted. "It tastes like…like…burned mud!"

Manuelo took a bite, too. "Yeccch! This is not Manuelo's authentic Russian-Rican stroganoff recipe!"

Chloe's eyes grew enormous. "Oh, no!" she cried out. "Maybe I defrosted the wrong Baggie!"

"Defrosted?" her mom repeated. "Chloe, what do you mean?"

Chloe glanced around the table sheepishly. "Um, well, I kind of have a confession to make…."

chapter
fourteen

Riley popped a handful of popcorn into her mouth.

"Hey, stop hogging the bowl," Chloe told her. They were sitting on the floor in front of the TV.

"Save some for your dad and me," Mrs. Carlson called from the living room couch.

The interview with Kendall Clark was about to air. Riley, Chloe, their parents, and Manuelo were waiting for the show to come on. After Riley confessed about her "designing" and Chloe about her "cooking," their mom and dad decided to come clean themselves—and informed Kendall that they were not powerhouse designers together anymore—all while Kevin the cameraman was filming.

Nobody knew what Kendall was going to do with that information.

"Shh, it's starting!" Manuelo said.

"This is going to be so humiliating," Riley remarked.

"But we'll be humiliated as a family," Mrs. Carlson

pointed out." She smiled. "All for one, and one for all. Right everybody?"

"Speak for yourself," Manuelo grumbled.

The commercial ended, and Kendall Clark's face filled the screen. "Welcome to *At Home with Kendall Clark*. Today, we're coming to you from the home of Jake and Macy Carlson, fashion designers extraordinaire…."

"Hey, I look good," Riley murmured.

"I look better," Chloe teased her.

"Shh!" Manuelo hissed.

[<u>Riley</u>: Would you believe that Kendall Clark decided NOT to air that footage of us—even after Chloe, Mom, and Dad spilled their guts on camera? Instead, she showed a straight interview, leaving Chloe, Manuelo, and me in the background. Mom and Dad looked totally creative and wonderful.]

[<u>Chloe</u>: Yeah. And Riley and I came off as loving, supportive children, which we are. Dad called Kendall's office right after the show to thank her. Kendall refused to speak to him. Instead, her assistant told him that Ms. Clark knew that we'd staged that whole fiasco to make her look bad, and she'd never interview the Carlson family again. I am so NOT upset about that.]

After the show was over, Mrs. Carlson turned to the girls. "Of course, you're going to have to apologize to your teachers about lying in class, that is," she told them.

Riley made a face. "We know."

"It'll probably mean detention," Mr. Carlson added.

"We're willing to take our punishment," Chloe said, hanging her head.

Mrs. Carlson turned to her husband. "Of course, we haven't exactly set the best example as far as honesty is concerned. We have to do better. Maybe we could take a seminar on the subject—families and honesty."

"We'll see," Mr. Carlson said.

The phone rang. Manuelo answered it. "Hello, Carlson residence." He glanced up. "Riley, it's Mr. Larry."

"Oh." Riley got to her feet and took the phone from Manuelo. She went into the kitchen. "Hey, Larry."

"I just saw the show," he told her excitedly. "But I'm not calling about that. Bob actually apologized to me— can you believe it? He said he realizes now that I was only in sewing class for 'babe-scoring purposes.'" Larry laughed. "Thanks, Riley! You held up your end of the bargain!"

"No problem," Riley said.

"Bob also said you told him that you found guys who sewed really hot. Does that mean you've finally decided to go out with me?"

"No!" Riley said.

"Okay, okay, just asking," Larry added quickly.

Chloe laughed when Riley told her that Larry had asked her out again for the thousandth time.

The doorbell rang. "I'll get it," Chloe said, jumping up from the couch.

She ran to the door and opened it. Standing there in all his sun-bleached glory was...Travis.

Chloe was totally surprised. She didn't think he wanted to speak to her ever again after she canceled their picnic date. "Hey," she said softly.

"Hey," Travis said. "Listen. I just saw the show, and I wanted to apologize."

Chloe started. "*You* want to apologize to *me*?"

Travis nodded. "I know now that you were telling me the truth. I shouldn't have gotten mad at you for not having time to go out with me. You had a lot going on with the TV show and stuff."

Chloe smiled. Things were working out with Travis, after all! And then she had an idea.

"Hey, let me make it up to you," Chloe said. "Why don't we go on that picnic right now? I'll hurry up and make some grilled cheese sandwiches, just like you wanted. I did promise to cook!"

Travis got a funny look on his face. He bent down and picked up something on the porch.

Chloe strained to see. It was a picnic basket!

"Um, I thought maybe I should do the cooking," Travis said, holding up the basket.

Chloe laughed and held out a hand. Travis took it and pulled her out the door.

"You are so right," she agreed.

mary-kate olsen ashley olsen

so little time

Chloe
and Riley's

SCRAPBOOK

What's the big deal? You cut the fabric...you sew the fabric.

Sorry, Larry. That outfit just doesn't work for you.

Here's a sneak peek at

Mary-Kate and Ashley
Sweet 16

A special three-part series.

BOOK 1:
Never Been Kissed

(available April 2002)

BOOK 2:
Wishes and Dreams

(available May 2002)

BOOK 3:
Going My Way

(available June 2002)

BOOK 2
Wishes and Dreams

Ashley and I were walking down the hallway at the end of lunch period when we ran into Melanie Han and Tashema Mitchell.

"Hey, you guys! We're *so* excited about your party!" Melanie said.

"Sending us updates about your sweet sixteen by e-mail is so cool. How'd you come up with that idea?" Tashema asked.

"Oh, it just, um—came to us," I said.

My sister and I exchanged a look. No one knew that the location of our sweet sixteen was a secret—because *we* didn't even know where we were having it! There were fourteen days and counting until our big party, and we still hadn't found the perfect party place!

But that was okay. I knew that Ashley and I would come up with something awesome—even if we did it with seconds to spare.

"So when's the next update?" Melanie asked.

"Soon," Ashley teased. "But we can't tell you when, because that would ruin the surprise."

"Can't you give us a clue? A teensy tiny clue?" Melanie begged.

"Not even one," I told her. "Just keep checking your e-mail."

"Okay, but the suspense is killing me," Tashema said before she and Melanie walked off.

I nudged Ashley with my elbow. "Sounds like our plan is working great!"

Ashley smiled. "You're right. No one suspects a thing!"

We turned the corner at the end of the hall—and nearly crashed into Rachel Adams.

"Hey, Mary-Kate. Hi, Ashley. I got your e-mail invitation—thanks!" she said.

"You're welcome," I told her with a smile. "Do you think you can make it to our party?"

"I'll be there for sure—and I *love* that the girls are inviting the guys. I'm asking tons of boys, so we should have enough to dance with and—"

I turned and looked at Ashley, whose face had gone completely pale. "Um, did you just say you're inviting *tons* of boys?" I asked Rachel. "You were only supposed to invite one."

Rachel looked at me with a confused expression. "Well, your e-mail said to invite *guys*. Plural," she explained. "So I thought I'd invite the guys' basketball team. Then I asked my older brother if he'd come along and bring a couple of his friends, because some of them are really cute."

"Yeah, um, that sounds great!" Ashley said. She started pulling me away. "I'm sorry, Rachel, but we have to run now. See you later!"

Ashley and I raced down the hall. I knew where we were headed. We had to get to the computer lab to check out the e-mail we sent.

"We didn't," I said as we ran.

"We couldn't have," Ashley agreed. We rushed into the lab and grabbed a seat at one of the terminals. Ashley signed on to our e-mail account in record time. She pulled up our "Sent Mail."

Suddenly, there it was on the screen: our latest e-mail update about our sweet sixteen party. Ashley ran her finger along the message until she got to the important line.

"Please invite the guys of your choice," she read.

"Rachel was right! It's *guys*—plural!" I wailed.

Several heads popped up from behind computer monitors as people strained to see what was going on.

"Mary-Kate," Ashley whispered, "the entire school is going to come to our party now. The entire city! We can't have a party for all of those people. What are we going to do?"

Reading Checklist

andashley

ingle one!

- It's a Twin Thing
- How to Flunk Your First Date
- The Sleepover Secret
- One Twin Too Many
- To Snoop or Not to Snoop?
- My Sister the Supermodel
- Two's a Crowd
- Let's Party!
- Calling All Boys
- Winner Take All
- P. S. Wish You Were Here
- The Cool Club
- War of the Wardrobes
- Bye-Bye Boyfriend
- It's Snow Problem
- Likes Me, Likes Me Not
- Shore Thing
- Two for the Road

- ❑ Surprise, Surprise
- ❑ Sealed With a Kiss
- ❑ Now You See Him, Now you Don't
- ❑ April Fools' Rules!

so little time

- ❑ How to Train a Boy
- ❑ Instant Boyfriend
- ❑ Too Good To Be True

- ❑ Never Been Kissed
- ❑ Wishes and Dreams
- ❑ Going My Way

Super Specials:
- ❑ My Mary-Kate & Ashley Diary
- ❑ Our Story
- ❑ Passport to Paris Scrapbook
- ❑ Be My Valentine

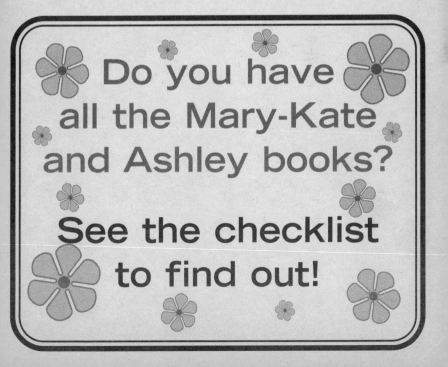